DOT & BEN

A 20th Century Love Story

PAT BACKLEY

DOT AND BEN

Pat Backley
www.patbackley.com

Paperback ISBN: 978-1-9911944-4-2
EPub ISBN: 978-1-9911944-5-9

Edited by Colleen Ward

Cover design and formatting by Formattedbooks.com

CONTENTS

ACKNOWLEDGEMENTS

This book, the third one in my ANCESTORS series, is dedicated to my parents, without whom this story could not have been written.

Whilst fiction, this book is based on their life stories. Most of it is absolutely true, but obviously, some other things I have had to imagine. I hope I have made my parents proud.

I would also like to thank my editor Colleen Ward, once again it has been a pleasure to work with her.

I dedicate this book to my beloved daughter, Lucy. It is her family history too, that I am proud and honoured to tell. While our ancestors no longer have a voice, I will make sure their stories are still told.

DOT'S STORY.
SURREY, ENGLAND
1958

Dot sat at the wooden table with a blank piece of paper in front of her.

The table had definitely seen better days. It was old and scratched, with great gauges running across the top, where years of careless use had ruined the once-pristine lacquered surface. Made of English oak, it had been varnished in the trend of the 1930s and 40s with a dark brown, shiny finish. She had always thought it was rather hideous, but it was all they had been able to afford when they first moved into the house.

She hadn't really minded at first. It had been an adventure to finally have a home and furniture of her own, away from the rather intimidating presence of her mother-in-law Lou. She had been so busy running the house and looking after two little ones at the time that she had barely noticed the shabby second-hand table. Most of the time, she had it covered with a nice clean tablecloth anyway.

But now, five years and three children later, the rosy glow had worn off and she seemed to notice every little flaw, in the house, in her husband, and in the wretched table.

She pulled the piece of paper towards her and began to write, in her beautiful copperplate hand....

"I have come to believe that poverty can drain you of any joy in life........."

How on earth had it come to this? Dot was at the point of wishing she could stick her head in the gas oven and end it all.

Of course, she never would follow through–not really–but she had certainly been tempted a few times lately. Especially when everything got so on top of her that she just couldn't think straight.

Like that poor woman, Sadie.

Dot had seen Sadie a few times in the street and always nodded a shy hello as she hurried past, but they had never really had a proper conversation.

Now, Dot regretted that. She regretted that she'd never bothered to take the time to get to know the young woman who, just last week, had hung herself from a tree, leaving a sad little note pinned to her shabby homemade cardigan.

Apparently, her husband had left her and her two small sons a few months before, and she had been trying to manage with no money or family support. The note said that Sadie knew her boys would be better off being adopted by some rich family who could take care of them properly.

Thinking about that poor soul, Dot knew she must stop crying and pull herself together a bit, maybe have a bath and wash her hair. She didn't want to be discovered looking unkempt and messy when Ben and the children got home. But for now, maybe she could just have a little wallow and shed a few tears?

She was so fed up being poor, counting every penny, trying desperately to pay the rent every week and feed her kids.

It was never meant to be like this. She had envisaged such a glorious future: a future free from war, rationing, and everyday worries about survival. She had never imagined she would end up like this, end up with a life of sheer drudgery.

She washed her hair in freezing cold water in the little bathroom sink, trying to get rid of all the soapy bubbles caused by the dishwashing liquid she had used. As usual, they had run out of proper shampoo; it never seemed to last long enough and there was no money to replace it until Ben gave her some more housekeeping money on Friday. There wasn't even any toothpaste left, she would have to make do with a handful of salt on her toothbrush instead. Dot was so sick of living from hand to mouth, from payday to payday. Never having enough to provide her little family with even the basics. How had it turned out to be so hard, such a struggle all the time?

She lived a rather miserable existence, trying to make ends meet all the time whilst putting on a brave face to the outside world and pretending that everything in the garden was rosy.

Sometimes it really felt like life would never improve, never get better for her and her children.

She had always been poor—she was used to going without—but this was much worse and she just couldn't see any end to it. Certainly it was nothing like the exciting golden future she had planned when she was a little girl.

BACK TO THE BEGINNING.
CAMDEN TOWN, LONDON
1920s

Her first memory was of lying under a green quilted eiderdown. It had been so comforting, almost as though a big friendly animal was cuddling her.

Daylight streamed in through the large window. It was only two o'clock in the afternoon, but as usual, her Grandma Martha, had insisted she needed a nap.

"You just pop off for a little snooze, my love. Then you'll have plenty of energy to play before teatime."

Three-year-old Dot didn't really mind, even though she hardly ever managed to fall asleep during these enforced afternoon naps. Instead, she enjoyed snuggling up under the covers and listening to all the sounds.

She could hear two women talking in the kitchen next door, the comforting sounds of her grandma chatting to her best friend, Olga.

Olga was an old Russian lady who, together with her younger sister Svetlana, shared the house with them. Dot loved them both; they had been part of her family her whole life.

Dot especially loved Grandma Martha.

Martha had been like a mother to Dot her since her own mum Lily died the year prior. Sometimes, Dot worried that she would forget what her mum looked like, so she would spend ages staring at the photo that was propped up in a frame on the mantelpiece in the kitchen. Then, she would look at herself in the mirror, trying to see if she bore any resemblance to the pretty young woman in the picture.

By now, Dot had almost forgotten the sound of her mum's voice.

She did remember that it was soft, gentle, and loving. Her mum had been so full of fun and laughter; it had been such an awful shock to them all when she had died, just two weeks before her 31st birthday.

The sound of the organ grinder in the street outside prompted Dot to leap out of bed and peer out the window. Her bedroom was on the middle floor of a three-storey Georgian house, so she could get a good view of the street below.

The organ grinder had always fascinated her. He was a wizened little man, his leathery skin tanned dark from all the hours he spent outside, summer and winter alike. He wore a uniform of sorts, a rather worn-out black thing with gold braiding on the jacket–something that looked as though it might have belonged to a soldier from the Boer War. Dot thought he was the most fascinating and interesting person she had ever seen.

He would come 'round every few weeks and stand in the street playing tunes on his barrel organ, while his pet monkey, dressed in a little sailor suit, would dance alongside, making the gathering crowd laugh at his antics.

It was a poor neighbourhood, so he didn't get much money in his cap, but he didn't care. He came from the mean streets of the East End himself, so he knew how hard it was for these folk. If he could make them smile, give them a bit of pleasure–a diversion from their dreary, difficult lives–he was happy to do that occasionally. For the rest of the week he would go out west, to Piccadilly Circus, and stand under the Eros statue. He always made a pretty penny there. All those toffs seemed to love him and his monkey.

"What on earth are you doing young lady, hanging out of the window like that? You'll catch your death of cold, and what will the neighbours think?"

"Oh Grandma, isn't it lovely? When I grow up, I'd like to learn to play the organ and get a monkey to dance for me. Then I could earn lots of money and Dad wouldn't have to work so hard."

Little Dot adored her father, Valentine George. In her eyes, he was the finest man imaginable: a war hero, a wonderful father. Not to mention, he could play the harmonica and the accordion!

Martha chuckled.

"Oh my little love, that son of mine doesn't realise how lucky he is to have such a lovely daughter. You are so like your mum, God Bless her soul. She was a kind-hearted girl too."

Martha's eyes clouded over as she spoke. They were all still in mourning for Lily. The house seemed so quiet without her.

Not that she had been rowdy, but you could always tell she was around by the sound of her tinkling laughter. She had been such a happy person, despite all the sadness she had suffered over the years. How they missed her.

Wiping away her tears with the corner of her rough calico apron, Martha held the little girl tightly in her arms.

"Why don't we pop downstairs, out into the street, so you can get a better look? I know that old monkey would be pleased to see you."

Dot's childhood was punctuated with lovely memories like that.

Of course, there were plenty of sad and difficult times too, but the little girl was determined to be happy, to make the most of every situation.

She lived in a house in Georgiana Street, Camden Town, with her father, Valentine George, her little brother, John, Grandma Martha, Olga and Svetlana, and her Uncle Albert, her dad's brother, who had lost an arm in the war, back in 1918. Downstairs in the basement lived her other relatives: Granny Sarah, her mum's mum, and her uncles, Dick and Harry.

Dot had been born in this house, in the very bed where her dad still slept, on the top floor. She had never known anything else—had never left Camden Town for even one night. But she had big plans.

"When I grow up, I want to be a famous artist and travel all over the world. Me and Uncle Albert can do it together, 'cos he's already famous."

Dot spent much of her time sitting at the old pine kitchen table, piles of paper in front of her, copying her uncle's work.

Albert was her dad's brother. He and Valentine George had both volunteered for the army as teenagers, back at the start of the war in 1914. Two young innocents who had never been out of the East End of London before really believed the government propaganda. They believed that they were fighting for King and Country, believed that they would help to make a lasting change in the War to End All Wars.

The brothers had returned to England much changed. They were no longer the carefree, bright-eyed young boys who had left, proud and cocky in their shiny new uniforms. At the end of it all, they were men, disillusioned with all they had seen and experienced out in North Africa. It had been a bloody war.

Due to his war injuries (in addition to a missing arm, he suffered greatly from shell shock and still had nightmares every night, reliving his time in the trenches), Albert didn't go out to work. Instead he used his talent as an artist, doing portraits. Luckily, it was his left arm–rather than the right one that he used to hold a paintbrush–that had been lost.

Initially he had just done the portraits for free, for their neighbours and friends, but now he sometimes went up to the West End and sat in Trafalgar Square or Piccadilly, where the toffs would pay him a pretty penny to make their likeness.

He loved teaching little Dot. She was a smart girl and picked everything up so easily. He only had to show her once how to draw something and she would produce a childish masterpiece. There were lots of them pinned to the wooden mantelpiece in the kitchen.

Dot grew up, contented and happy with her lot.

There were a few dramas, of course. Even a little girl growing up in the bosom of a loving family was not immune to the tragedies of life.

Losing her mum at such a young age was just awful, especially as it had happened so suddenly. One day her mum was there, laughing, joking, and hugging her tightly as always, the next she was gone.

For a long time, Dot expected her to come back. They all said she had "gone to Heaven," so surely she would come back soon. Heaven couldn't be that far away.

She had hated seeing everyone so sad when it happened. Until that point, she had never seen her big, strong dad cry; afterward, it seemed like he cried all the time. Her Granny Martha cried a lot too. Dot often saw her wiping away her tears on the old beige calico apron she always wore.

She sometimes caught Olga and Svetlana deep in conversation, muttering away in their native Russian tongue, both with tears running down their cheeks. Of course, they hastily wiped them away and enfolded the little girl in their arms once they noticed her nearby, desperately trying to shield her from their sadness.

Downstairs was even worse. If she ventured down there to visit Granny Sarah, her mum's mum, she almost always found her in floods of tears, weeping and wailing.

"Why did He take my lovely girl? She never hurt a fly. Should have been me gone instead. I'm just a stupid old woman. No-one would miss me."

The little girl didn't really know what to do, how to comfort them all. So she just wandered around the house, going up and downstairs, trying to cheer them all up. Often it worked, and just the sight of the pretty little girl desperately trying to lessen their grief was enough.

But at night, when she was safely tucked up in bed, they would talk.

"Our Lily was one of a kind. They'll never be another one like her."

"What on earth are those poor little kids going to do without a mother's love?"

"I don't suppose our Valentine will ever get over it. She was the love of his life; there will never be another like her. I don't reckon he'll ever love again."

"I'm a bit worried about our Dot starting school. You know how unkind kids can be. Someone's bound to start teasing her about not having a mother."

Little Dot's father was not privy to most of these conversations. He was too wrapped up in his own grief, trying desperately to retain some semblance of normality for his two motherless children whilst dealing with his own loss.

He had loved Lily so deeply. Since that first day he had met her, all through the dreadful war years when they had been parted. Then, they had enjoyed just a few gloriously happy years together before she had been so cruelly snatched away from him.

Thank goodness he had his mum Martha and the others living in the house with them. At least it gave him a bit of space to grieve alone. He would spend interminable hours in the mews stables where he worked, nestling up to the horses, his tears dripping onto their shiny coats. He tried so hard not to cry in front of his children. At least in the darkness of the old stable block, he could release all his pent-up feelings and allow the tears to flow.

"Oh Lily, I don't think I can do it on my own. You were such a wonderful mother. I just don't know what we're going to do without you."

He remembered the awful time when little Dot was just one year old and had been so close to death. They had all been frantic, not knowing what to do for the best, and then Rose, his sister, had decided to call the doctor. He and Lily had been putting off doing so, hoping that their little girl would get better, that some miracle would happen without them having to spend sixpence they could ill afford to get the doctor to call to the house.

"Look, Valentine. Me and Cyril have got a few quid put by. We were saving it for our holidays, but we'd much rather use it to help little Dot get better. I'd never forgive myself if something happened to her."

So, the doctor came to the house, took one look at the ashen-faced little girl who was writhing in agony, and declared that it was far too late to get her to hospital. He told them all that he would have to operate there and then to have any chance of saving her young life.

He took off his jacket, rolled up his sleeves, and demanded that they scrub the pine kitchen table.

Lily and Valentine were both weeping as their little girl was lifted gently onto the table, at once thoroughly cleaned and covered in old white sheets.

Neither of them could bear to watch when, after sedating her with chloroform, the doctor laid out his shiny equipment, ready to perform the emergency operation. All they could think about was how they had lost their first two children in infancy. Surely their only living child wasn't going to be cruelly snatched away, too.

Lily gently touched her swollen belly, feeling the new baby inside kick. This was Dot's little brother or sister, who was almost ready to be born.

The operation seemed to take forever. The family all stood silently in the kitchen, watching the doctor. Luckily, he was highly trained and skilful, not like some of the quack doctors around.

Rose had offered to act as his nurse. Although she wasn't trained, she was calm and sensible, which were two traits that were much needed under the circumstances. She handed the doctor his instruments and kept checking on Dot's breathing. It was the worst possible situation for a loving aunt to be in. Lily's brothers, Dick and Harry, had come up from downstairs to act as porters, gently lifting Dot onto the table, then holding her down once she was asleep–just in case her little body jerked during the operation.

Eventually, it was done. The doctor washed his hands under the old kitchen tap, put on his jacket, pocketed the money that Rose offered (the price had gone up of course, as it turned out to be rather more than a routine home visit), and took a last look at the little girl who was lying on the kitchen table, drowsy, but still alive.

"Well, she should be fine in a week or two. Just keep her warm and give her plenty of broth. She won't be able to stomach more than that for a while. Good job you called me. These

umbilical hernias can be dreadful things, especially in such a young one. Make sure you keep the wound clean. I will pop back in a day or two to see how it's healing. No further charge. Oh and by the way, she hasn't got a belly button now."

Once Dot was older and the wound had healed, leaving a noticeable scar, she was rather proud of her lack of a belly button. It made a great story, and of course, the little girl loved to embellish the tale, recounting the gallons of lost blood and surgeon's knives sparkling in the gas light of the little kitchen!

It took them all a while before they could relax while eating at the table after that. All they could visualise was the sight of their beloved little girl so close to death. But they had no choice. Life had to go on. Being poor didn't allow you the luxury of wallowing for long.

Luckily, the new baby was made of strong stuff; he emerged noisily into the world just a few weeks after Dot's ordeal. She was just over a year old herself–still a toddler re-ally–but instantly, she became another mother to the little boy, adoring him from the first moment she laid eyes on him.

They were all so happy for a while. At last, Valentine George and Lily had the little family they had dreamt of for so long. Losing their first two babies would always be a great sad-ness, but at least now, they had the future to look forward to.

Sadly, their future was not to be long lived. Just two years after little John was born, Lily died.

She had been tired for a while, but just put it down to running a home and looking after two active children. She lost her appetite and so began to lose weight. The pain in her back wouldn't go away and although she was secretly worried, she tried to carry on as usual.

She couldn't afford to waste money on seeing a doctor and certainly didn't want to make a fuss.

Finally, Valentine insisted on taking her to the hospital. Like most poor people, they only went to hospital as a last resort–only if they were really sick or had broken a bone. They both hated the imposing old brick buildings of St. Pancras Hospital. Part of the building had originally been the old workhouse, and like most people of their class, they and their ancestors had lived in terror of "going on the parish"–becoming a workhouse inmate.

By the time they got back to Georgiana Street that evening, they were both in despair. The news they had been given at the hospital was sad and shocking. It seemed that Lily had chronic kidney disease and the doctors could do nothing for her. They predicted that, at her young age of 30, she might have another year–at most–to live.

Sadly the doctors miscalculated the prognosis. The precious young woman, a much-loved wife and mother to two small children, died just four months later, two weeks before her 31st birthday. She was buried in a grave at Finchley Cemetery, finally able to be alongside her two dead babies.

CAMDEN TOWN–
THE EARLY YEARS.

Children have a great capacity to live the life they are born into without questioning it too much.

Dot knew that she was different from her friends.

She was motherless for a start, although she was always surrounded by love. Love from her dad, her little brother, her two grannies, and all her uncles and aunties.

But none of her friends lived with Russians!

Olga and Svetlana had lived with the family forever, moving with them from the slums of the East End to the relative comfort of the rented house in Georgiana Street in Camden Town.

They had helped Grandma Martha when she was a young, struggling widow. They had taught her how to sew, which brought in a few much-needed pennies, and had helped her to care for the children. After some time, the three women began a small dressmaking business. Finding out that it had always been her ambition to be a seamstress, they had trained Lily, Dot's mum, to help them. She had been a wonderful addition to their little team; now that she was gone, they missed her sunny chatter, as well as her beautiful sewing. The little room they used as their sewing room and showroom was so quiet without her.

Dot had never known another life. She had been born in the house they all lived in and enjoyed the freedom of running from one floor to another, usually being sure of a loving welcome at whomever's room she happened to appear in. Everyone in the house loved her and her little brother John passionately and tried very hard to make up for them losing their mother.

So, until the age of five, Dot lived a happy existence.

They were a poor, but loving family. They had a roof over their heads, the men all had steady, albeit not very well paid, jobs, and the women were busy all day, keeping the house clean, looking after the kids, and running their sewing business. Like most working class people, they often had to "rob Peter to pay Paul"–using some of the rent money to buy food, but at least none of the men wasted their money on drink or gambling.

Granny Sarah, however, after turning briefly to religion following the death of her daughter, Lily, finally reverted to her old ways. She took to spending all her spare money on snuff and gin, even pawning her sons' suits every week to satisfy her addiction.

"Oh for Gawd's sake, Mum. Why are you going down this path again? We all miss our Lily, you know we do. But drinking yourself to death isn't going to bring her back, you know."

"Harry is right, Mum. Those kids need us all now. You can't help them if you're always off your head. I still don't understand

why you gave up on the religion. You seemed much happier when you were going to that mission church every Sunday."

Sarah was ashamed. Ashamed that she was letting everyone down, ashamed that she couldn't seem to keep away from the gin. No wonder everyone called it Mother's Ruin. It was certainly ruining her life.

"Also Mum, we've noticed that lately, you seem to be a bit hard on our little Dot. It's not fair, you know. She loves you. We don't understand why you seem to have turned against her so."

She knew her sons were right. Lately she had been finding it hard to be kind to Dot. Somehow, every time she looked at her little granddaughter, she was reminded so much of Lily. Her Lily, her little girl who had been so cruelly snatched away. She knew it wasn't fair, but somehow she just couldn't seem to help it. It was so much easier to be kind to little John, Dot's brother. Looking at him didn't make her heart break over and over.

When Dot turned five, her life changed. She was sent to school, the old ragged school in Camden Town. Suddenly, she was no longer safely in the bosom of her large, loving family. Instead, she was thrust out into a different world–a world of wooden ink-stained desks, blackboards, and bullying.

She had been so excited on her first day. Leaving home, hand in hand with her Grandma Martha. She was wearing a starched white pinafore, button boots, and a big, brand-new white ribbon tied in her hair. She felt just like a princess. She didn't care that the pinafore was second- or probably third-hand. Her granny had bought it down Camden Market and had washed and starched it until it was bright white. She didn't know where the button boots had come from, they were well worn and didn't really fit very well, but by the time her dad had spent ages polishing them, they gleamed like brand-new ones. The white ribbon in her hair came from Olga. It was a leftover piece from a dress she had just finished making for a lady in Belgravia.

Unfortunately, nothing in her young life had prepared her for the cruelty of the other children.

"Oh look, here comes that silly girl who hasn't got a mum..."

"...And her granny is always drunk."

"Wonder where she got those old clothes from. The pawn-brokers, I expect."

These comments came from the older girls. Girls that Dot had often seen in the street or at the market.

She went home that afternoon in floods of tears.

"Now, my girl. You listen to me. You're just as good as the rest of them. We may not have as much money, but your dad and uncles work jolly hard to look after us. Being poor is nothing to be ashamed of."

She was still upset when her dad came in from work. He was a gentle, caring man, and it broke his heart to see his beloved little girl so upset. He held her tightly in his arms and let her sob. If only his Lily had been there. She would have known how to comfort their girl.

The next day, Dot woke up with a tummy ache. She begged and pleaded with her grandma to let her stay at home.

"I hate that place. If you make me go there again, I'll probably die—or run away. Uncle Albert, please tell Grandma I don't have to go."

Albert looked down at the little girl. His precious niece, the little girl he adored. The closest thing he would ever have to a child of his own. Having lost his arm and been shell shocked in the war, he knew he wasn't attractive to women any longer.

"Oh, darling girl. I wish I could keep you here at home forever. It would be such fun, but we would get into trouble for not sending you to school. And anyway, how on earth are you going to get to be cleverer than me and your dad, if you don't do your lessons? They will teach you how to do sums and write letters, and they'll tell you all about the world—all the different countries and the people and animals that live there. You'll end up so smart that you'll be able to come home and give us all lessons! I hear they even teach you drawing and reading, maybe even poetry.

Little Dot reluctantly returned to school; by the end of the first term, she loved it. She tried really hard and ended up finishing top of the class in nearly every subject, but her favourites were reading, writing, and geography. She loved learning about the world. These lessons opened her mind to a whole new way of life, a life far away from the crowded streets of Camden Town.

Despite being so smart, she was never a very confident little girl. She was still bullied sometimes by the older girls, especially about the way she walked. She was a little bow-legged and sometimes her knees really hurt, especially when she was running around trying to keep up with the other children at playtime.

Having seen a few doctors at the hospital, it was finally decided that she had to have an operation. It seemed that, as well as having rickets (a disease common among the poor, working classes at that time), they discovered that both her kneecaps were in the wrong place. They proposed to put her under anaesthetic and move them.

Apparently the operation was pronounced a great success, but she had to spend several months afterwards with both legs encased in plaster of Paris. She hated having to be carried everywhere, no longer being able to run up and down the stairs as she had always done. Her dad rigged up a baby's pushchair to take her weight–luckily, she was only a slight little scrap of a girl, rather small for her age–and her friends would knock at the door, asking if they could "take Dot for a walk."

The whole episode did nothing for her confidence, but at least the teachers sent work for her to do at home so she didn't fall too far behind in her schoolwork.

By the time she was seven, her legs had healed and she was back at school full time. She loved her lessons even more than before, having been away for almost a year. The teachers were delighted to have her back, this studious, hard-working little girl. She was a girl from a rather impoverished background, but she had big ambitions.

1929–A TIME OF CHANGE.

1929 proved to be a year of great change for Dot's family.

They lost Svetlana, following a very severe seizure. She had suffered epileptic fits for many years, but none of them had been as serious as this one and it was very unexpected. The house fell into deep mourning; it was too soon after Lily's death and they all grieved.

Then, Valentine George contracted rheumatic fever and they thought they were going to lose him too. He was carted off to hospital, where he spent weeks hovering between life and death.

It was almost as though he had given up, as if the pain of carrying on without his beloved Lily was too much.

In the end he rallied and was sent to a convalescence home in Bognor Regis. It was thought that the bracing sea air would speed up his recovery.

He spent several weeks down there, returning to London looking fitter and healthier than he had in years. He even looked as though he had put on a little weight. Martha was delighted to see her son looking so well.

"*Mum, I've got something to tell you.*"

"*Oh yes, love. What is it? By the way, I thought I'd do some nice sausage and mash for our tea. The kids love it, and I know it always used to be your favourite. I got some really nice sausages from that butcher on the high street. We're so happy to have you back, son, we missed you so much. Little Dot hardly slept last night, she was so excited at the thought of seeing you.*"

"*Actually Mum, I've met someone.*"

They were alone in the kitchen.

"*What kind of someone, Valentine?*"

"*A lady. Her name is Elizabeth. Elizabeth Silver. She's a widow, lost her husband three years ago.*"

"*Oh, I see.*"

It had never occurred to Martha that her son might meet someone else. He had been so devastated when Lily died. Somehow, she had always thought he was a one woman man, the kind of man who would only love once in his life. But looking at him now, she realised she was obviously wrong. There was a twinkle in his bright blue eyes that she hadn't seen for many years.

"*Did you meet her in Bognor?*"

"*Yes I did, Mum. She was convalescing too, so we kind of just got chatting every day when we were outside getting fresh air. I'm planning to go and visit her on Sunday, now we're both back in London.*"

"*Where does she live?*"

"*In Battersea. She lives with her mum and dad, her old granny, and her two sons.*"

"*Two sons? How old are they?*"

"Tommy is 14 and Harry is nearly 12."

Martha's heart sank. It sounded like he knew a lot about her family already. She just hoped he wasn't going to do anything rash; he still wasn't truly over Lily.

Little Dot fell in love with Elizabeth Silver the minute she met her.

She had been invited to Georgiana Street to tea the following Saturday. Everyone crowded into the first floor kitchen, where a buffet lunch had been laid out on the old pine table under a clean and starched white cloth. The event took place at the very table where little Dot had been operated on all those years ago.

"Everyone, this is Elizabeth. And these are her sons, Tommy and Harry."

The two boys looked very uncomfortable. They would much rather have been with their mates, riding their bikes or playing football down the rec. Instead, their mum had dragged them here, across the river, to meet up with some strange new family.

"Pleased to meet you all, I'm sure."

She spoke in a quiet voice, rather cultured, with no trace of the East End.

After lunch, when all the adults were sitting around drinking cups of tea, Dot perched herself on a cushion on the floor, right next to her dad's new friend, Elizabeth. She listened carefully to all the talk around her, never once taking her eyes off the woman. She studied her clothing, the elegant pale-green satin dress with a fashionable dropped waist. The matching cloche hat, now removed, sitting on the small table beside her. The pearls around her slim neck. The tiny gold watch.

"*Dot, do you like school?*"

She suddenly realised that the beautiful creature was addressing her.

"*Umm, yes I do.*"

"*And what are your best subjects? Do you have any favourite lessons?*"

By the end of the afternoon, the little girl was besotted. She didn't think anyone, apart from her own family, had even taken such an interest in her before.

"*Dad, are you going to marry that lady?*"

BATTERSEA, LONDON.
1930s

Martha had been wrong when she thought that Valentine was a one woman man. Just a few months later, he announced that he had asked Elizabeth to marry him— and that she had accepted.

"Isn't anybody going to congratulate me? I thought you'd all be pleased."

"If you get married, does that mean I can call Ms. Silver 'Mum?'"

"Yes it does, Dot. If you'd like to."

He was so relieved that at least his precious daughter seemed happy at the news, even if the rest of his family didn't.

Dot was thrilled. It sounded like she was going to be getting a new mum, which would be wonderful. Of course, she didn't really know Ms. Silver very well, but she seemed like a nice lady. It would be so good to be the same as all her friends and have a mum of her very own.

Later that evening, when everyone else was tucked up in bed, Martha tackled him.

"Oh son, what are you thinking? You haven't known the woman for five minutes. Are you really sure about this? I know you miss Lily, but you might be jumping from the frying pan into the fire here. What do you really know about her and her family? Isn't she a bit old for you? Don't you think her boys might resent you for taking the place of their dad? Where on earth are you all going to live? There isn't really room for everyone here, but I daresay we could squeeze them all in if we had to..."

Valentine's bride-to-be was getting a similar grilling from her family.

"But what do you really know about him? He hasn't got much of a job, just working in some removal company. He can't earn a very good wage doing that."

"Does his family live as well as us, or do you think he's just a gold digger, thinking you are a woman of means?"

She held her ground.

"He is a good man and his children are so sweet. Especially his little girl, Dot. She is such a dear little thing, so sweet and affectionate. You know I always wanted a daughter."

"Oh Lizzie, wanting a daughter is no reason to marry a man you hardly know. A man much younger than you who doesn't even have his own home and probably can't afford to support you all properly."

Despite the less-than-enthusiastic response from both their families, Valentine and Elizabeth were determined. On a chilly spring afternoon, when there was still a trace of snow on the grass, they were married at the Evangelist Mission Church on Wandsworth Road, with a reception that followed at the old Red House Inn on Stewarts Lane. This was Lizzie's dad's local spot–the pub he and his mates drank in every Friday night when they got their wages.

After a brief honeymoon in Bognor, in a little B&B guesthouse just off the seafront where they had first met, they returned to London.

"Oh Mum, do stop crying. It's not like we're going to the other side of the world. You can come and see us anytime you like. Lizzie will always make you welcome."

It had been decided that Valentine and his children would move to Battersea, into the house Lizzie already shared with the rest of her family. It would be a bit of a squeeze, but she had absolutely refused to move to Camden Town.

"Oh love, I do hope you understand, but I'm a bit too old to move in with my mother-in-law and the boys are so settled in their schools. Moving to Georgiana Street just isn't a good idea."

The day they moved was terrible. The only one who was excited was little Dot. She was going to get a mum at last!

Everyone else was in tears. Martha, Olga, Albert, and Granny Sarah. Even little John started crying, just because everyone else was.

Dick and Harry, Lily's brothers, were loading up the cart, and even they had tears in their eyes.

"Are you really sure about this, mate? We can easily unpack it all. Maybe Lizzie will change her mind? It seems jolly unfair to expect those kids to leave us lot and the only home they've ever known. Their mum would be turning in her grave if she could see it."

Valentine was not unmoved by their pleas. If the decision had been up to him, of course he would have stayed in the bosom of his family, where he knew his two motherless children would be loved and cared for. But he had made his bed; he'd married the woman and now he had to make the best of it.

"Ms. Silver, can I call you 'Mum?'"

Elizabeth Silver, better known as Lizzie, smiled down at the little girl.

The others were still outside unpacking the cart, but Dot had rushed into the house, so excited about meeting the woman who was going to change her life. She was wearing an old dress, a grey and pink calico one, but in her hair she had a pink, shiny ribbon that Grandma Martha had given her that morning.

Martha had struggled to hold back the tears as she brushed the little girl's hair.

"Oh my little love, we want you to look smart today, going to meet your new relatives properly for the first time. Of course they will all love you, but it doesn't hurt to look as pretty as you can. I've popped a few extra ribbons in your bag, nice, coloured ones that will go with everything. That way, every time you wear them, you can think of me and Olga in our little sewing room."

Martha felt as though her heart was breaking. She had never imagined that Valentine and his children would ever leave her. She thought they would all stay in Georgiana Street together, forever. Until her dying day.

And now they were going. Over the river. To Battersea. It might as well have been the end of the world, as far as Martha was concerned.

Although Valentine had promised he would visit often, and of course she would always be welcome there, she knew it was the end of an era. She would no longer see her son and grandchildren every day or have them sitting at her kitchen table for every meal. She would no longer be able to listen to Dot's enthusiastic chatter all day long or hear her little voice singing as she wandered around the house.

Now, they were gone.

"Ms. Silver, can I please call you 'Mum?'"

Lizzie looked at the little girl, and her own eyes filled with tears. This poor, motherless little girl was so desperate to have a mother.

"Of course, love. I would be delighted if you did."

"Can our John call you 'Mum' too?"

Dot had always been very protective of her little brother. John had been born when she was just a toddler herself and from the moment he had arrived into the world she had adored him. After the tragic death of their mum Lily, she had taken him under her wing completely and had become a little mother to him. Always hovering, making sure he was well and happy.

"Of course he can, love, but I think he's a bit more interested in his new brothers than he is me."

It was true. John already idolised his step-brothers, Tommy and Harry. As soon as they had arrived at the little house in Battersea, he had gone rushing off, chasing after the two bigger boys as they rode their bikes around the park opposite the house.

"Oh no, Ms. Silver, I mean, Mum. I'm sure he loves you just as much as them. He's just excited about having big boys to play with; we never had any other kids at home, you see."

Lizzie winced as she heard the catch in the little girl's voice. It was going to be so hard for her, having to adapt to her new life in this new household, when she had spent her entire life in the bosom of her own family.

Later that evening, when all the children were safely tucked up in bed, she spoke.

"Valentine, love."

"Yes, my darling?"

"I've just been thinking about your little Dot. I'm a bit worried that she won't find it easy to settle here. It's so different from the life she's known."

"Oh Lizzie, she'll be fine. She loves you already, and the rest of your family are really nice to her. I'm sure it won't take her long at all to settle."

He was right. Children are very adaptable, particularly if they have no choice, and in no time at all, Dot became used to her new surroundings. She missed everyone at Georgiana Street of course, but having a new mum was wonderful.

Lizzie took her out every day. It was still the school holidays, but they had already been to Sleaford Street School to register her as a new pupil starting in September. The next week, they planned to go shopping for her new school uniform, a satchel, and some stationery, but in the meantime, they were going to visit the dressmaker's.

Dot stood as still as she could while Sybil, the dressmaker, measured her with an old wooden ruler.

"My God, Lizzie, she's a tiny little thing. How old did you say she was?

It won't take much fabric to run her up a few nice dresses. In fact, I can even use your offcuts, if you'd like. Seems a shame to throw away all those nice bits of material."

Dot ended up with four new dresses. She was absolutely thrilled, especially because they matched the ones her new mum had. Now, everyone would know she belonged.

Battersea was a bit different from Camden Town.

Lizzie's family lived in New Road, Battersea (later to be renamed as Thessaly Street), in a three-storey brick built house in a terrace of about twenty. The houses had been built some 50 years earlier–during the late Victorian era–so were typical of that period, with sash cord windows, metal railings around the small front gardens, and large chimneys on the roof that seemed to be constantly billowing out smoke from the multiple fires burning inside. Most of the houses on the street were divided into rooms; very few of the ordinary, working-class people who lived there could afford to rent a whole house for their family.

There were public houses on every corner of the street, and in fact, probably on every corner of almost every street in Battersea. Dot had never seen so many pubs in her life. She wasn't that fond of them, really. She had seen too many drunken men, staggering home after a skinful on a Friday night. Back to their poor homes and their poor, hungry families. She had seen the misery that drink caused. Her own Granny Sarah had often been drunk. Drunk on gin, snuff, and misery. Dot had vowed that she would never touch the stuff, that she would remain teetotal for all her life.

Occasionally, she would go with her dad to Uncle Tom's Cabin in Wandsworth Road, next to the railway arch. It was something of an institution. She loved the old metal signs on the brick wall, advertising Camp Coffee, R. White's Ginger Beer, and Watney's Pimlico Ale, but she especially loved the little café's name. She imagined that the first owner, the original *Uncle Tom*, must have loved one of her favourite books–written nearly a hundred years ago by an American lady called Harriet Beacher Stowe–to have named his little café after it. It wasn't really a proper café, just a little tea stall, but as Dot munched on her slice of cake and drank her ginger beer, it seemed like the most glorious place in the world- even if the calm was frequently shattered by noisy trains running overhead.

In fact, Battersea was quite a noisy place altogether. Noisy and a bit grubby from the constant smoke belching out from the new power station. The red bricks on the houses nearby were already blackened and sometimes the smog was unbearable, but apparently the Battersea Power Station was going to be a great asset. Although it would burn more than 200 tons of coal per hour, it would eventually electrify many of the city's homes and businesses, taking away the need for gas lighting.

Dot had always been used to sharing a house with extended family, so it came as no surprise to find her new home full of Lizzie's relatives.

She became especially fond of her new step-great-grandmother, a tiny lady who seemed to be rather ancient. She was quietly spoken and always wore long black dresses and a bonnet, in the style of the late Queen Victoria. Her little room on the ground floor seemed rather exciting to little Dot; it was so dark and gloomy, stuffed full of the old lady's treasures. Cabinets full of old china, glass domes with dried flower arrangements inside, and a huge aspidistra plant on the little table in the bay window.

She was as different from Grandma Martha in Camden Town as it was possible to be, but she filled a very apparent gap in the little girl's life. In time, Dot came to love her dearly—not as much as she loved Martha of course, but on a day-to-day basis, she was always there and she was kind.

The house had a big garden at the back, surrounded by a high brick wall. In no time, Tommy and Harry had taught their new step-brother and step-sister how to climb onto it to watch all the trains as they whizzed past.

The railway arch was just at the end of the street, and after passing the little bakery shop where Lizzie bought their bread every day, there was a turning that led to Sleaford Street. This was quite a small street with old cottages lining one side and a school on the other.

Sleaford Street School.

Here the boys and girls were segregated, the boys' classroom upstairs and the girls' below.

After just a few weeks, Dot was happily settled there. She loved the little school, but mostly she loved her teacher, Miss. Todd. The middle-aged woman was a natural teacher, knowing how to draw the best out of each of her young students, and she was a natural storyteller. The girls under her care learnt so much. She read them the classics, poetry, prose, and poems they would remember and be able to recite all their lives.

Lizzie was very affectionate towards her new step-children.

She particularly loved Dot. Having always wanted a daughter of her own, she went out of her way to ensure the little girl was happy. She bought her new dresses and leather button boots, lace hankies and pretty ribbons for her hair. Sometimes, they would walk along New Road towards Battersea Bridge, passing little cottages and small shops, and Lizzie seemed to know everyone.

"This is my new daughter, Dot" she would say with pride.

Dot was thrilled. Having a mum was just as wonderful as she had always imagined it would be. Of course she missed everyone at Georgiana Street terribly, but her dad took her back to see them every few weeks. She wished they would come and see her–she really wanted to show them her new school and everything–but apparently Granny Martha thought it was too far away, too hard to come across the river, even to see her precious girl.

Sometimes they would go to the mission hall and watch the Magic Lantern show.

Going in the other direction, towards Lavender Hill, they passed a few small cottages, several large, grand houses, a fish shop, and a blacksmith's forge.

Lizzie belonged to an evangelical mission in Wandsworth Road called Springfield Hall. Every Sunday evening she took Dot along with her to listen to the choir. The little girl was rather in awe, not just of the beautiful singing, but because in her imaginative little mind, they seemed like angels, all dressed in white.

The children were supposed to go to Sunday school there too, but some Sunday afternoons found Dot, John, and their step-brothers standing on the railway bridge watching the trains whizz by whilst sucking on sweets they had bought with the pennies intended for the church collection. Still, as long as they got home at the usual time, they were confident their mum and dad would never find out!

On sunny summer evenings, Valentine and Lizzie would take the children into Battersea Park to listen to the band. For once in her little life, Dot felt rather posh as she took her seat in the bandstand. Most people just had to sit around on the grass. She loved the music, the smart costumes the bandsmen wore, the whole rather magical atmosphere. But most of all, she loved having a mum at last. She snuggled up closer to Lizzie and whispered, *"Thank you. This is the best, most happiest time of my whole life. I love you, Mum."*

Her three brothers weren't very interested in school, considering it something of a waste of time. They just wanted to grow up, get jobs, and have fun.

Dot on the other hand, flourished.

Now that she had a mum of her very own, she could concentrate on learning all about the world. She wasn't going to be like those silly brothers of hers, she was going to make something of her life. Something big and adventurous.

Of course, when she was younger, she had always planned to be a great artist and go travelling around the world with her Uncle Albert. He earned his living drawing portraits of people. Sometimes he set up his easel in Piccadilly Square, under the watching eye of the Eros statue, sometimes he tried his luck in Trafalgar Square instead. She had always been amazed at his ability to do such great work with only one arm (he had lost the other fighting at Gallipoli), but when she praised him, he always laughed.

"Oh no, my little love, I'm not that talented. Just lucky all the toffs feel sorry for me 'cos I lost my arm in the war."

What Dot really wanted to do now was become an artist and writer, travelling all around the world, sketching as she went. She was also rather fond of books and poetry, and of course, these inspired her hugely. Maybe she could even become a famous gardener–after all, the weedy little red geranium plant her dad had given her for her birthday was thriving. It seemed to like living in the window box at the front of the house, on show for all the neighbours to see. In fact she had begged her dad to buy a few more so that she could fill the window box on the other side of the house too, but he had smiled sadly.

"Oh love, I wish I could, but money doesn't grow on trees, you know. And even down the market those plants cost a bit. One day, when I'm rich, I'll buy you a whole garden full, I promise."

Dot didn't mind. One day, when she was all grown up, she would buy her own plants and have the most beautiful garden in the world.

She loved school, loved learning new things every day. Reading new books, learning new poems, geography and history, reading and writing. She even liked arithmetic.

"Old Meg, she was a gypsy, she lived among the moors. Her bed, it was the brown heath turf and her house was out of doors."

Valentine and Lizzie smiled. They had had their tea and now Dot was giving them a little show, telling them all about her day at school.

"*That's nice, love. Did your teacher write it?*"

"*No, Mum. It's by a very famous poet called John Keats. He lived hundreds of years ago. Shall I say the whole thing?*"

"*And with her fingers old and brown she plaited mats of rushes...*"

After the little girl had gone to bed, Valentine sat down to write a letter to his mum. How he missed them all. It was okay here in Battersea, but sometimes he wondered if he had done the right thing, moving over the river, away from everyone and everything he had ever known.

"*...You won't believe how well Dot is doing in school. They say she's very gifted and she's nearly always on top of her class in reading, writing, and art. She drew a picture of the old king the other day, in his uniform with all his medals. Mum, she got a really good likeness. Do tell our Albert, he'll be so pleased that she's following in his footsteps.*"

Dot continued to thrive in Battersea. Having a mum of her very own at last was so wonderful.

Lizzie was marvellous with the little girl. She took her to the London Zoo, where they were both fascinated by the monkeys and spent ages watching their antics. Then they moved onto the lions' enclosure and the little girl whispered in her ear, "*When we get home, Mum, I'm going to tell you another poem, a really good one that Miss. Todd taught us last week, all about lions.*"

"*There's a famous seaside place called Blackpool, that's noted for fresh air and fun, and Mr. and Mrs. Ramsbottom went there with young Albert, their son.*"

Lizzie was standing at the sink, washing the dishes after tea time.

"*I thought you said it was about lions, love?*"

"*It is, Dad. You just have to be patient.*"

After what seemed like ages to Valentine, who was threatening to nod off in his chair if she didn't get a move on, the lions were finally mentioned.

"*There were one great big lion called Wallace, his nose was all covered with scars. He lay in a som-no-lent posture, with the side of his face on the bars.*"

Dot continued quoting the poem, which she had now learnt almost by heart. As the story got more dramatic she flung her little arms around.

"*The keeper was quite nice about it, he said, what a nasty mishap. Are you sure that it's your boy he's eaten?*"

By the grand finale, her parents were open mouthed, both at the rather shocking story and Dot's ability to recite it from memory.

"*What? Waste all our lives raising children, to feed ruddy lions? Not me.*"

"*Oh, Lizzie. I really wish we could afford to get our girl a decent education. To send her to a really good school. She's obviously really bright, I just hate to think that our poverty will hold her back.*"

By the time Dot was due to take her eleven-plus exam she was thriving, doing really well at school and in her home life. She had made new friends and Battersea now seemed like home.

Most especially, Dot missed her Aunty Rose, her dad's sister. Rose had always been such a huge part of the little girl's life, taking an interest in everything she did and trying to fill the gap that Lily had left when she died.

Rose was very different from the rest of the family.

She was loud, dramatic, and outspoken. She firmly believed that women were just as good as men and luckily, she had married a man, Cyril, who supported this wholeheartedly. He was quiet, she was not. He was calm, she was not. He hated dramatics, she thrived on them. But they also shared many common traits. Both were kind, loving, and fiercely loyal.

Cyril came from a rather wealthy family, old money. When he had announced that he was in love and intended to marry Rose, a girl from an ordinary family (at that time they lived in the East End slums in very poor circumstances), his parents had been horrified. They refused to meet the girl and announced that if he was insistent on this foolish plan, they would have no choice but to disinherit him entirely.

Cyril had been determined. He knew he had found the love of his life, this pretty, feisty young woman. He still couldn't believe she had agreed to become his wife. He remembered the first time he had seen her, back in 1917. He had popped into Lyons Corner House for a cup of tea and a toasted tea cake one day, and there she was—the most beautiful creature he had ever seen. Gliding from table to table in her black dress and starched white apron, a waitress from heaven!

His tea went cold and the toasted tea cake lay on his plate, both completely untouched, he was so mesmerised by the sight of her.

Of course he didn't talk to her that day, he was far too much of a gentleman to accost her in that way, but he went back two or three times every week for the next month.

"I say, Miss. That was a jolly nice teacake… I wonder if I could take you out? To the pictures maybe? Anytime that suits you, of course. Any time's good for me. Or maybe you'd rather go out for a meal? Or perhaps that's too much of a busman's holiday? Maybe just a walk? Or the music hall?"

He was blushing and stuttering very slightly, something he hadn't done for years, and he was rabbiting away, like someone possessed. Normally he was very calm and assured, but there was just something about this girl.

"Glad you enjoyed your meal, sir. We aim to please. Although, I daresay that you might have enjoyed that teacake a bit more if you actually ate any of it."

He was entranced. Not only was she beautiful, but she was funny and feisty as well. Quite unlike those rather insipid debutantes his mother was constantly introducing him to.

A few months later, they were engaged. Rose had met her match, a partner who would love and support her, but not demand that she change, give up her job, or become a boring housewife with no opinions other than his. It was a match made in heaven, and neither of them cared about him being disinherited. They both knew that the love they had was worth more than all the riches in the world.

Another hero of young Dot was Amy Johnson, the brave woman who, in 1928, had flown herself in a small plane all the way to Australia and back. Dot had been so thrilled when, one summer evening, she and John were tucked up in bed and her Dad had rushed in excitedly telling them to get dressed.

"Hurry up, you two. We're going to see Amy Johnson being escorted into London after her flight home from Australia."

It was getting dark when they arrived at Battersea Bridge. The crowds were so excited. Suddenly, there were great cheers and along came an open-topped car with a police escort. Sitting in the back and waving to the crowd was the famous Amy Johnson herself. Valentine was so excited that he jumped onto the footplate of the car to shake Amy's hand. The policemen just smiled at his enthusiasm. Everyone was so excited to see their hero in person.

That summer, everywhere you went, loudspeakers were playing the song for Amy:

"Amy, wonderful Amy. I'm proud of the way you flew. Since you won the pride of every nation, you have filled my heart with admiration…"

Lizzie realised early on that her little step-daughter had big dreams and ambitions, so within her limited budget, she did her best to satisfy the little girl's curiosity.

The two of them often went to the Grand Theatre at Clapham–usually when the boys were going to the cinema and refused to have a girl tag along with them. Dot didn't care. She loved her brothers, but she would much rather have a bit of proper culture than watch those horrid cowboy movies the boys loved so much.

For their summer holidays, Valentine and Lizzie would take the kids to Southend for a few days. The boys wanted to spend all their time on the beach, but Dot thought it was too hot, so she always sheltered under a little umbrella and watched them frolicking in the chilly sea. She much preferred the Kursaal fairground and the shows. Sometimes, when the tide was out, Valentine would walk them out to see the remains of an old German warship that had been there since the Great War. Dot wasn't very fond of the sea; on these walks she was constantly checking that the tide wasn't coming in too quickly for them to get safely back on the beach. If she was honest, she didn't really enjoy the water at all. Like many kids brought up in London without easy access to beaches or swimming pools, she had never learnt to swim. She could do a doggy paddle of sorts, but nothing that gave her any real confidence in her ability not to drown.

Sometimes the adults would pop into a pub for a quick pint and the kids were allowed to sit in the pub garden, nursing their bottle of pop and packet of Smith's crisps. Dot was always careful to undo the little blue twist of salt inside the packet slowly, gently sprinkling it over the potato crisps. She thought it was very exciting, such a treat–almost as good as the arrowroot biscuits she sometimes got as a pub treat instead. Mind you, she was also rather fond of the sweets she bought with her penny pocket money every Saturday... treacle toffees and satin cushions were her current favourites!

"Now come on, Valentine. Are you sure little Dot's doing all right? That girl has such a good brain, so much potential. Look how she won that award in the London Safety First competition.

That essay of hers must have been really good, 'cos there were kids entering from all the schools in London—even the posh schools. And she won that poetry competition last year, too. I'm just worried that she's not going to get the chance to really shine, especially if you and Lizzie insist on dragging her out to live in the sticks before she's even had the chance to sit her eleven-plus. You know, her teacher said she would pass with flying colours, she's so bright. Maybe, if you and Lizzie are happy with the idea, she could stay here in Camden with mum, and Cyril and I could drive her over the river to school every day. It's only for a few months, after all."

"Oh Rose, don't nag. I know you want the best for Dot, but Lizzie and I went to see her teacher and she said that the new school would be fine, that she could sit her eleven-plus when she got there. Apparently, she's so smart she can easily pass wherever she is. We want the best for her too, you know."

Valentine spoke a bit sharply, because in his heart he felt that his sister was right. He had already dragged his children away from Camden Town and the family and home they grew up in; now he was doing it again. Well actually, that wasn't strictly true. There was a new move in the works, and it was all Lizzie's idea. She had made the choice without even consulting him. He had come home one day to the news that she had had put them on the list for a new council house, miles away, in the countryside in Morden. Now it was happening. They had been offered a newly-built house with three bedrooms and a garden. It sounded great, but it was Lizzie's dream, not his.

He looked around the familiar kitchen in Camden. They were all sitting–he, Rose, and Martha–around the old pine kitchen table. The table that had seen so much life. The table he had rested his weary head and wept on for hours after Lily died. The table where the doctor had done an operation to save baby Dot's life. The table in the house where his children had grown up, so different from his family's earlier life in the slums of the East End. He looked at his sister, feeling guilty as he noticed the tears pouring down her pretty face. He hated being responsible for making anyone sad, especially Rose and his mum. She was crying too.

"Oh, son. If I thought it was the right move for you all, of course I'd be happy. But you know how I feel."

Valentine did know. His mum had been very vocal about him getting married again. It wasn't so much that she didn't approve of Lizzie, she just thought it was the wrong decision for him and the children.

And maybe she was right.

He was happy enough, but he did miss Camden, the camaraderie of his mates, and living within the bosom of his big, loving family. He missed feeling like he really belonged. Lizzie's family members were nice to him of course, but it just wasn't the same. However, he also knew he had made his bed, now he had to lie in it. There was no going back.

MORDEN.
1933

In the end, moving had been a difficult transition for everyone.

Going to the countryside was something of an eye opener for this city-born and bred family. It took them a long time to get used to being surrounded by green fields and farms, rather than the crowded streets and hustle and bustle of London. The three young boys loved it, of course, as they could get on their bikes and disappear for hours exploring their new surroundings. The other three, however, took longer to adjust. Dot, Valentine, and Lizzie all missed the busyness of the city—the old cobbled streets, the sounds of horses, buses, and trams. The countryside was so quiet and dark at night; it was all so different.

The house was lovely, a brand-new solid brick construction in a terrace of twelve identical ones. The whole neighbourhood was made of distinctive red brick, and each house had a little porch over the front door. Lizzie and Valentine's was the end one in the row, so they had a bigger garden than the rest. They made big plans to grow their own vegetables, maybe even plant an apple tree or two.

Lizzie missed her family in Battersea. Moving to the country had seemed like such a good idea, a new start for them all. But once she was actually there, she realised it wasn't what she really wanted. She loved playing house and planting a few flowers in the garden, but her heart wasn't really in it. She missed London.

Still, it had been her decision, now it was up to her to make it work for all of them.

She knew that Valentine hated having to make the long journey back up to town every day. He didn't complain, of course, he was far too much of a gentleman for that, but she felt a bit guilty when he had to leave before six every morning, not getting back 'til seven every night looking a bit grey and tired. Still, at least he wasn't working at that removal firm anymore. Rose had somehow wangled him an interview in Old Bond Street, in the dispatch room for Gieves, the naval gentleman's outfitters. Luckily he seemed to be thriving there, so that was one less thing to worry about.

Little Dot, now aged eleven, was blossoming.

She loved the new house, especially the inside toilet. It was such a luxury not having to go outside in the middle of the night or use one of those horrible porcelain chamber-pots under the bed. In fact, her step-mum, on discovering the inside toilet in the house, had insisted on collecting together everyone's old chamber-pots and using them in the new garden to grow plants! Dot was a bit embarrassed seeing them all lined up on an old bench outside, but the boys said she was just being an old, soppy prude! She didn't know what a "prude" was, and rather than ask, she looked it up in the school dictionary.

"Prude—a person who shows extreme modesty, especially in sexual matters."

Now, she even had a bedroom all to herself. It was quite small, just big enough for her bed, a chest of drawers, and a little chair, but there was a cupboard with hooks inside to hang her clothes. Best of all, she didn't have to share it with her brothers!

She loved her school in the countryside: No. 1 Girls' Central School, Morden. It was only a fifteen-minute walk from the new house, and she had already made some new friends there. It was much bigger than her old school which she didn't mind, because it had much better facilities. There was a big library, a concrete playground, and a huge grass playing field. There was also a big assembly hall where everyone gathered for hymns and prayers before school began each day. But the best thing of all, in Dot's eyes, was the art studio.

Dot still loved art. She had spent her early childhood watching Uncle Albert draw his portraits, and now she was producing lots of work of her own. Some of her pieces were even winning prizes. She had been so proud to receive a certificate from the Royal Drawing Society saying that she had passed her exam with honours. Her dad had it framed and it was now hanging proudly in the front room.

The only thing that Dot was sad about was that she never got to take her eleven-plus exam after all. Despite school officials promising that it would not be a problem, when she arrived, they announced she was too late, that the names for entrance had already been sent off and hers could not be added. Lizzie went to see the headmistress to plead her case, but to no avail.

Despite this disappointment, Dot thrived. She was sad not to have a nice eleven-plus certificate like her friends, but she was smart and could easily hold her own in class.

Dot amazed her new English teacher by quoting poems by heart, poems like Meg Merrilies by Keats and William Wordsworth's one about daffodils:

"I wandered lonely as a cloud
That floats on high o'er vales and hills,
When all at once I saw a crowd,
A host, of golden daffodils..."

At home, she was happy to help her step-mum with the chores. At this time, Lizzie had got a little part-time job just a few mornings a week in an office, and of course, Dot's dad was away all day, working in the city.

Her three brothers were useless, of course. They didn't want to help around the house; they just wanted to eat their meals and escape outside on their bikes.

All the washing was done in the bathroom sink with a wooden scrubbing board and big bars of soap. After rinsing, the clothes and bed linens had to go through the old mangle, which stood outside on the concrete slab by the back door. Using the mangle was Dot's job and she took great pleasure feeding the dripping wet items through the two big rollers and watching all the excess water come out underneath. She was only a tiny little thing, but was very determined. Although it was hard work to turn the handle, she found it quite relaxing. It reminded her of all the times she had helped Grandma Martha do the wash in Camden Town. She felt the tears welling and sniffed loudly as she reminisced.

Although she had adjusted to loving her new life in the country, she missed her family back in Georgiana Street. She missed sitting at the old pine kitchen table sharing a meal with everyone. She missed drawing with her Uncle Albert and going to the market with Grandma. She missed Aunty Rose popping in, missed listening to all her wonderful stories about the people she had met or the plans she had. Rose was little Dot's heroine.

It was such a shame that none of them came down to Morden much. She knew it was a long way, but she did wish she could see more of them. They were her *real* family, after all.

Still, she was SO happy to have a mum of her own again at last. She knew that Lizzie loved her and she absolutely worshipped her in return.

It was just a shame that lately, Tommy and Harry didn't seem to be getting on too well with her dad. She had heard lots of raised voices, late at night, when she was supposed to be fast asleep.

She never saw the letter that Valentine sent to his mum:

"They're nothing like the little lads I took on when we got married. They were so sweet then, seemed really happy to have a step-dad, but now I'm actually not so sure. We've had a few blow ups recently, silly things like me asking them to put their

bikes away properly in the shed rather than just leaving them lying on the lawn and squashing the grass. Of course their mum takes their side, says I'm being unreasonable and that I should leave them alone. I'm sure it's all just a phase. Once they're over this difficult stage, I hope it will go back to how it was. Honestly, I'm not sure if this move to the country was the right thing for them. They were older than my two, more established in their London lives. I think they miss all their mates."

Three months later, it all came to a head. The blended family had spent a lovely Christmas in Morden. Rose and Cyril had driven everyone down from Camden Town and they had spent a couple of very happy days celebrating the holidays together.

Valentine wrote to his mum again.

"I just wanted to say how much we loved having you all here at Christmas, it was such a happy time. We really missed you after you left, the house seemed awfully quiet.

Unfortunately, after you all left, we had a huge falling out with the boys. Tommy said he and Harry were fed up with me still treating them like kids now that they are both grown up and working. It all blew up a bit. I'm afraid I lost my temper and said some things I probably shouldn't have, and the outcome was that they packed their bags and left. They said they were going back to live in London. Lizzie is distraught of course, but I keep telling her they'll be back... that she is such a good mum, so indulgent, and they know where their bread is buttered. They take up a lot of space and don't really contribute anything. Lizzie is a bit soft and still doesn't charge them anything for their keep."

MOTHERLESS AGAIN.

It had been just a few weeks since Valentine had sent that letter to his mum. The house had been very calm since the boys had left, and although Lizzie seemed rather quiet, he truly thought it was all going to be okay. The boys would come back eventually with their tails between their legs, he was sure of that. And in the meantime, he was enjoying having his wife to himself.

Dot skipped home from school one day with her friend Rosie. They were practising for the school's annual Sports Day. It was months away–not 'til June–but they had decided if they started training now, they would be in good shape when the time came.

Dot was very happy. Since this particular day was a Tuesday, she knew they would have her favourite for tea: liver and bacon. Her mum always made that on Tuesdays.

She waved goodbye to Rosie and continued on down the street. How lucky that her new best friend lived on exactly the same road as her! Their mums even got together sometimes for a cup of tea and a chat, although that wasn't happening so much lately. Lizzie had been a bit quiet since the boys had left home.

Dot approached the front door and stuck her key in the lock. She didn't usually have a key because her mum was always there when she got home from school, but this morning, as she was putting on her school uniform–navy-blue knickers, white vest and blouse, and blue pinafore dress (which some people called a "drill slip")–her mum slipped a piece of thin white ribbon around her neck. Dangling from the ribbon was a front door key.

"I have an appointment today, love, so you might have to let yourself in."

The minute she walked in the house, Dot knew something was wrong. It wasn't just that the house was so quiet, it felt entirely *different* somehow.

She continued into the front room and gasped. Everything was gone. The only stick of furniture remaining was her dad's old Windsor chair.

Maybe they had been burgled? Whatever would her mum and dad say?

She went into the little kitchen and found a note pinned to the cupboard:

"I'm sorry. I can't stay here without my boys. They say they're never coming back, so I have to go. Please Valentine, don't try and change my mind. Just take care of little Dot and John."

In a daze, Dot wandered around the house. Every room was empty. Everything was gone except for the kettle, three plates, three cups, three knives, forks, and spoons, a tin of tea, and a bottle of milk. All the beds and bedroom furniture had seemingly disappeared. Lizzie had left just a couple of threadbare towels in the bathroom, along with the children's few toys and all their clothes.

Dot sat on the stairs and cried. She cried until there were no more tears left. She had been so happy having Lizzie as her mum, and now it was over. Obviously her new mum, whom she loved and adored, hadn't really loved her after all. Otherwise, why would she have just walked out and left? Just like that, without saying a word. Dot didn't even get to say goodbye.

Once the little girl had calmed down a little, her mind went into overdrive. She had always been protective of her little brother, and her first thought was that she didn't want him seeing this. She didn't want him to ever be hurting like she was now.

She slowly walked back outside, closed the front door behind her, hung the key back around her neck, and walked to the end of the road. She knew John would be home soon. He was always later than she was, dilly dallying with his mates. She decided she had to stall him; she just couldn't let him go inside to see their empty house.

"We'll have to play outside 'til Dad gets home. I haven't got a key."

"Where's Mum? She's always at home. I'm starving. Can we break in and get some bread and jam to keep us going?"

She hated lying to her brother, but she just didn't know what else to do. Luckily it was a dry and not-too-chilly spring day, and the hours passed quickly as John and his friends played endless games of cricket on the little green while Dot sat quietly under a tree, trying not to cry.

"Oh look, Dot, there's Dad coming down the road now. Shall we run up and meet him?"

"No John, he'll be tired. Let him get indoors and get his slippers on before you start pestering him."

It seemed like forever passed before their dad came out of the house and beckoned them over. He seemed to have aged at least twenty years and Dot could tell he had been crying.

STARTING OVER.

The first night without Lizzie passed in somewhat of a blur for all of them.

They cuddled up together on the old Windsor chair: father, son, and daughter. Weeping copiously. Valentine couldn't hide his distress, not even to spare his precious children. He was so shocked. Although he knew that Lizzie missed her boys, he had never imagined she would leave. Not like this, with no discussion or no explanation. Just that scrappy little note.

At some point that evening, there was a gentle knock at the door. Everyone leapt up, hoping it was Lizzie returning to them.

Sadly, it was just Mrs. Pratt from next door. Apparently she had seen Lizzie driving off with everything in a van, aided by Tommy, Harry, and her dad. They had all come down from Battersea to help her move.

"Hello lad. I'm so sorry for your troubles. You and those kiddies don't deserve it. I can't do much, but here are some blankets and a bit of food to keep you going."

Valentine, Dot, and John spent a sad, sleepless night lying on the cold lino in the front room, each covered by the thin woollen blankets their neighbour had so kindly lent them. There had been a bit of coal left in the shed, so they made a fire in the grate, which kept them a bit warm for a few hours.

Dot wanted to stay at home the next day. She couldn't bear to go to school and face all her friends, who were bound to ask questions.

As much as Valentine wanted to keep his two precious children with him and never let them out of his sight again, he knew he had no choice.

"Oh, my little love. I am so sorry, but you have to go to school. I need to go to work this morning, and then I'll try to sort everything out. I can't bring your mum back, but I promise you will both have a bed to sleep in by the weekend."

Dot's father was as good as his word. His boss was very kind. When he heard the sad story, he gave Valentine a loan to buy some new stuff. He left work early and went down to the second-hand shop, getting three beds, a couple of chairs, a table, and some sheets and blankets.

He wrote to his mum in Camden Town.

"Oh Mum, I just can't believe it. I thought she was better than this, just leaving without saying anything to my face or having a discussion. She never even mentioned having the thought of ending things between us, and certainly never mentioned she was thinking of leaving.

The kids are heartbroken, especially little Dot. She really loved Lizzie and was so happy to have a mother like all her friends. John was most upset when the two boys stormed off the other week; he looked up to them both so much.

Luckily, Lizzie left the kids' clothes and their few bits and pieces–not that they've got much–although Dot has got some pretty little dresses that Lizzie insisted on having made for her. I really thought she loved that girl like she was her own, but I guess I was wrong? I can't believe she's left us, I thought we were happy. I was happy, I really thought she was too.

Oh Mum, I just don't know how we're going to get through this. Dot is heartbroken. She and I just can't seem to stop crying. John seems happy enough as long as he's got a bit of food in his belly and is allowed to go outside to play with his friends.

Sorry to be so melancholy. I guess I just have to pull up my socks and get on with it. I wish we'd never left Camden Town. I wish I'd never married her."

Dot, a tiny little girl already, seemed to shrink even more in the weeks and months following Lizzie's departure. She barely spoke, apart from when she was safely at home, and school became difficult.

"Is it true your mum left because you were so naughty?"

"Maybe she never really loved you; after all, you were only her STEP-DAUGHTER!"

"My mum says that blood is thicker than water."

"Fancy losing two mums, that's a bit careless!"

Of course, she had no choice but to carry on. Her dad and brother needed her. So, at the tender age of just eleven, Dot found herself caring for the family home. She cooked and cleaned as soon as she got back from school. She made sure John did his homework and ate the dinner she had lovingly prepared for him before he went rushing out to play football with his mates.

Being so busy was something of a solace for the little girl. When she was home alone for such long periods waiting for her dad to return from work, she had a chance to think, to come to terms with her emotions and loss. It forced her to grow up very quickly–there was little time for much wallowing. She was now the one who had to keep her family together.

After a year, wounds began to heal.

Dot was enjoying school again; in fact, she was flourishing. Her mind was like a little sponge, she so loved learning. Her teachers were amazed. They knew how hard her life had been since her step-mother left, knew how hard her home life had become, and yet, she still soaked up all the knowledge she could. Her favourite subjects were English, art, and history, but she also loved geography and learning all about the world.

"One day, Miss, I'm going to travel the world, see all these exotic places. Nothing's going to stop me."

The teacher looked down at the girl who was speaking. Her little face was full of freckles and her fingers were covered in blue ink from dipping her pen into the inkwell on her desk. She was sitting in the front row of the classroom, which was full of old wooden desks with lift up lids and inkwells. A colourful room where every wall was full of posters and students' artwork. A room that was designed to inspire young minds. At the front of the classroom stood the teachers desk, larger than the others. It held a pile of books and a box full of white chalk that the teacher would use to write on the big blackboard:

"Always have an open and inquisitive mind."
"Always aim for ten out of ten."
"To travel is to experience life."
"Whatever your station in life, you can always move on."

Dot was ambitious. She knew–just knew–that once she was grown up, her life was going to be good and exciting. It was just a matter of time. She only wished either of her mums were still around to see what a great success she was going to be.

Her dad had been delighted with her school report.

"Dot works well in class, her conduct is very good indeed. She is an extremely good practical worker, especially in needle-work. Her drawing is very good and she works with great care. She deserves her honours pass in the external art exam. She has worked steadily all year. Her manners are quiet and she is reliable. Although she is inclined to be nervous, she has no need to be. She has worked very well this year."

One day she got home from school as usual, tidied the house, and made John an early dinner of sausage and mash so that he could go and play with his friends while it was still light outside. She planned to save hers so she could have it later, when her dad got in from work.

A letter had arrived, and she was dying to know what it said. They rarely got any post–except for bills or a letter from the family in Camden Town. Dot didn't recognise the writing on this one. The postman must have delivered it just that afternoon, as it had been sitting on the doormat when she got home.

She was so excited that she made her dad open it almost as soon as he got in the door. He only had time to take off his hat and coat and put on his slippers before she made him sit in his old chair in front of the roaring fire. Dot had become very good at laying a fire in the last year; she did it just as Lizzie had taught her: little sticks of firewood first, then screwed up bits of newspaper, and finally, a bit of coal on top. It had taken her a few weeks before she perfected her technique, but now she could get a roaring fire going and warm up the little room before her dad got home from work every day. The only thing she hated about it was that her hands ended up filthy from touching the newspaper and dirty black lumps of coal.

"Dear Valentine,

I am sorry to have to inform you that my dear niece Lizzie, your wife, died last week. As you know, her heart hadn't been good since she had that rheumatic fever, and they think it was complications from that that killed her. I also think she felt guilty about leaving you all like that too. She never really came to terms with it. She was a good woman at heart and never meant to do you all any harm. And she really loved little Dot. I do hope you are all getting on okay.

Regards, Alice."

Dot cried for days after they received this letter. Now, she would have to face the truth. Her step-mum was never coming back. Until that moment, the little girl had harboured a hope that Lizzie would return, would say she was sorry for leaving them, would want to come back.

Valentine was worried. It seemed so cruel that his dear little girl was having to go through so much pain again. He cursed Lizzie, but then felt bad for doing so. He wrote another letter to his mum, the only person with whom he felt able to share his thoughts.

"It's been such a rough year, but I'm glad to say the kids seem to be doing okay these days. I was so worried about my Dot. She just seemed to fade away after Lizzie left. It hit her so hard. First she lost her own mum, then her step-mum, whom she idolised, just abandoned us all.

But I mustn't speak ill of the dead, right? It was such a shock when we got the letter saying Lizzie had died. I did feel sad when I heard, Mum. I really loved that woman. It was much worse for my little Dot. She must have been bottling up all her feelings, 'cos when I showed her the letter she burst into tears and didn't stop crying for two days.

I think, maybe, 'til that point, she had been hoping that Lizzie would come back to us someday. It broke my heart to see her so upset; she's usually such a bright and happy little thing."

Time is a great healer, of course. We never forget the dreadful pain of losing someone we love, but in time, we get used to not having them around anymore. They become a wonderful memory, forever lodged deep within our hearts.

By the time Dot's 14th birthday came 'round, she had become a fine young woman—wise beyond her years. Valentine mentioned her in another letter to his mum.

"Dot has now left school. She didn't want to leave really, but we couldn't afford for her to stay on. Her dream was to go to art school or even university, but I think she now realises that people like us can't do those things. I think some of the girls at her school come from rich families, so maybe that's where she got the idea a while back? Anyway, she says she is happy to train as a tailoress instead, if I can manage to find her a position. The only trouble is that she's left-handed, so I don't know if I'm going to be able to get anyone willing to take her on. I'm going to start chatting to everyone in all the little tailors workshops in Soho where I collect stuff. Maybe one of them will be able to help? In the meantime, she's doing a good job keeping the house going and looking after John while he finishes his last few months at school. She's like a little mother to him. He doesn't have any ambition or any idea what he wants to do. I'm hoping he might find a job locally.

Oh Mum, I don't know what we would have done without Dot. She is such a sweet, loving girl and has really kept our little family together since Lizzie left. Not much of a life for such a young one though; I feel so guilty that she's had to take on so much."

Despite it all, Dot, the little girl with big dreams, thrived.

It wasn't the life she had hoped for or dreamt about, but at least it was a life outside the confines of her home, away from the day-to-day drudgery. She loved getting up early and going on the Underground train to London every day. She usually spent the whole journey with her head in a book. Reading was her solace, a way to experience the world–a world she really hoped to explore for herself one day. For now, she had to be content with just reading about it.

Her Aunty Rose, her absolute heroine, had always told her: *"Women are just as good as men. There's nothing we can't do if we put our minds to it. Just think of all the sacrifices those suffragettes made so we could have our freedom today."* She had even given Dot a book about it: *The Intelligent Woman's Guide to Socialism and Capitalism* by George Bernard Shaw.

The years passed. Suddenly it was 1939, and the world was on the brink of war.

Valentine continued to write to his mum every week. Neither of them had telephones at home, so it was the only way of keeping in touch.

"What do you think of the latest news? It's all a bit worrying, isn't it? While it's all very well for old Chamberlain to say that the government "emphatically disapproves of what Germany is up to in Austria," it's not looking good when they've started issuing us all gas masks. That speech he made about the Munich Agreement and "Peace for our time" worries me, too. I overhear lots of the naval bigwigs who come to Savile Row for their uniform fittings; they all say another war is inevitable. I'm scared for my Dot and John if there is another war. They're both old enough now to be called up."

DOT'S ARMY DAYS.

The war started in 1939, and it changed everything for ordinary people. First, the blackout was introduced, and one had to get used to walking along darkened streets at night. Most people who had gardens were issued Anderson shelters, which had to be half-buried in the garden and used during air raids.

Things were pretty quiet to begin with, but the first time the air raid sirens sounded, everyone dived for shelter. When the real Blitz started, things became quite hectic. Dot would come home from work, make a flask of tea and some sandwiches, and go into the shelter as soon as the sirens started. Sometimes, the family would go up to watch the air fights. On one particular night, a bomb landed at the bottom of their garden; as it had not yet exploded, the whole street was evacuated in the middle of the night. They had to quickly gather a few possessions and go along to a reception hall. By the morning, the bomb had exploded and everyone was allowed home, uncertain of what they would find when they got there. Luckily, Dot's house was intact, apart from a few cracked walls. The houses opposite, however, were completely destroyed. It was an anxious time. No-one ever knew if their home would still be standing after a night in the shelter.

Food rationing would become another worry, but because everybody was sure the war would be over "in a few months" initially, they took it all in their stride.

Then, as the fighting dragged on, everyone over the age of 18 had to register. Anyone on that list could be called up to fight.

Looking back sometimes, Dot thought the happiest part of her life was when she was in the army–back in 1940. She had only been 19 years old when she volunteered. All the men had already gone to the front, many never to return. It was a sad, difficult time, but somehow there was still an air of optimism around; surely, that monster Hitler would be defeated soon.

The old Jewish men she worked with all thought she was crazy when she enlisted.

"But why, my little one, don't you just stay here safely with us? You are such a good tailoress, we will miss you and your fine sewing. Why don't you just find a nice boy to marry and have a baby? Then they won't be able to send you off to war."

Later on, she could still remember how sad she had been saying goodbye to the other tailors at the little sitting in Soho–the place she had worked every day since she was 14. They were like another family to her.

They had all been shocked when Dot, the tiny little thing she was, first turned up in an oversized woollen overcoat all those years ago–their *"new little kipper."*

None of the tailors thought she would last, a young girl in a tailors' workshop full of old men. A young girl with no experience of sewing... and left-handed to boot.

Mr. Capp, the owner of the workshop, had only agreed to take her on as a favour to her father. Valentine had been dropping into the workroom in Soho for several years, collecting handmade suits and overcoats that were destined for the clientele of the posh menswear stores in Mayfair.

Throughout the years, over cups of strong, steaming coffee, Mr. Capp and the other tailors had learnt about Valentine's traumas, including the death of his first wife and the desertion by his second. He never complained, but rather told the sad tales in a chatty way. Informing, not seeking pity. When he mentioned one day that his daughter, his precious, motherless little girl, was desperate to be a tailoress, Mr. Capp's heart melted. Even though he knew there was no way a young girl could cope with the delicate work or the rough environment.

Luckily for everyone, Dot had proved them all wrong.

After just a few months in the workshop, she had won their grudging respect. Dot had copied the men as they sat cross-legged on the floor, carefully watching them work. Within a few weeks, she was producing scraps of amazing work–tiny, even stitches that were almost invisible to the naked eye. Of course, most of the time, she was just a skivvy, popping out to Berwick Street Market when the tailors wanted something to eat, sweeping the floor, or tidying up the rolls of fabric piled up on the old table. She loved to stroke the fabrics, feeling the softness of the velvet or the harshness of the Harris Tweed beneath her fingers.

After some time, the men had presented her with a special silver thimble. She had been puzzled initially because it was not filled in at the top, like the ones her Granny Martha and Olga used in their little shop. Instead, the top of her thimble was open. At first, she kept forgetting and pricked herself many times, but gradually, she learnt to do as the tailors around her were doing and use the side of the thimble to push through the heavy fabrics as she sewed.

Sometimes, she had to deliver the finished garments to Savile Row or Hanover Street herself if they needed to be rushed and the usual porters–like her dad–were busy with other jobs.

Often, Dot could be seen leaving Soho, marching down Regent and Oxford Streets and heading to the posh stores in Mayfair. People would stop and stare at the sight of the tiny little girl, wearing her oversized overcoat with her puny arms weighed down by garments. Sometimes there were so many piled up that she could barely see over the top.

Dot remembered those early days so well. She had been so excited to have a real job. Of course, it was hard. She was the only girl–young or old–in the workroom, and she knew that some of the older tailors resented her presence. They couldn't understand why old Capp had taken her on at all, a mere slip of a girl with no experience. Why, she wasn't even Jewish!

But five years later, they were all, every last man, devastated to see her go off to war. They had all grown so fond of her, she was almost like a daughter to them. And of course, with their training, she had turned out to be the most marvellous tailor. Nowadays, they got her to do all the fancy work, the jobs that required something extra. All the items were sewn completely by hand, there was not a machine in sight in that workroom. The only thing resembling a machine was the ancient old boiler in the corner that they all huddled around at lunchtime, trying desperately to warm up their tired, arthritic fingers.

Their little Dot now sewed outfits for aristocrats, princes, and kings.

"Don't be sad. I'll be back, just as soon as we've dealt with old Hitler."

Hitler–the man who would end up sending so many of their relatives to their deaths in Nazi Germany. The old men smiled sadly in the workshop. How could this young girl, their Dot, possibly manage to do away with that monster?

THE WAR YEARS.

Dot's war years were, in her own words, *"a marvelous time."* A time of freedom, laughter, and fun. Strange words to use to describe wartime, but to the young motherless girl from London, her new life *was* marvellous. She was living with lots of other women, some as young as her, but most of them a little older and more worldly wise. Her eyes were opened very quickly. From living a rather sheltered life at home with her father and brother, she was thrust into a gloriously feminine world—a world she had never been lucky enough to experience properly before.

The girls on her searchlight site became her family. They were all in this dreadful war together with one common aim: to get rid of Hitler and his army, an army that was threatening their very existence in a green and pleasant land. Their fears were very powerful things that brought out the very best <u>and</u> the very worst in them.

Obviously, the army bigwigs at the top knew how dangerous life was on the searchlight sites. It was common knowledge that several sites like Dot's had been completely wiped out, killing all the women, but of course they were forbidden to discuss such things, for fear of damaging the war effort. *"Careless talk costs lives."*

Dot was enlisted into the Auxiliary Territorial Service (ATS) at the end of 1941. With the war escalating, the military realized that some of the harder, more dangerous roles back home would have to be filled by women in order to release men to the front lines to fight. Having passed all the tests and examinations, Dot was sent to York to do her initial training; from there, onto Norton Manor Barracks in Taunton, Somerset. This was the regimental camp of the R.A. Light Ack-Ack (Searchlights).

They had never had female soldiers stationed in the barracks before, as manning searchlights was considered hard and dangerous work–totally unsuited to women. Dot and her new friends were given intensive training before going out to man the actual searchlight sites. It was never publicly known that many of these dangerous sites were run completely by women; the War Office felt it might affect public morale. The women became known as *"The War Office Babies."*

Dot's first site was at Barton-le-Clay in Bedfordshire, and there were twelve women running the site. They all had to learn every job so that they could lend a hand whenever and wherever it was needed. They had a Lister to generate power to the searchlight, but only Tilley lamps for lighting the small barrack rooms. The sergeant had a small, private hut while the other women shared two mission huts. There was a small cookhouse, rec. room, and washroom, but the outside toilets were very primitive and the women had to empty buckets into a cesspit. There was no running water, but a water cart came once a week to refill the tank situated on the roof of the main hut.

During the day, the women did site and equipment maintenance. In the evenings, as soon as it was dusk, they had to be ready at a minute's notice to man the searchlight. At first, they just had a sound locator to locate the enemy planes, but they soon had radar equipment fitted as well. The women quickly got used to having very little sleep. All their equipment–including their camp beds, searchlight, and generator–had to be ready to move to a new site at any time.

Something that made the women very angry was the fact that the men's sites had a Lewis gun, and each man was equipped with a rifle. The women had nothing in the way of weapons. They asked a visiting officer what would happen if any enemy parachutists landed on their site. "How are we supposed to defend ourselves?" They got this rather stupid reply:

"Use your womanly wiles and lure them into the kitchen." Obviously, the men at the top still thought their lives were worth less than their male counterparts.

They were on another site in Watford when the second front started in June 1944. Dot was acting DC (Detachment Commander) that day and had to organise the move to a new site in Kent. This became known as Doodlebug Alley, as the enemy had begun to send over unmanned missiles–V1 and V2 rockets. It was very frightening, as one never knew when or where they would land.

On 8 May 1945, the war was over. That day, the women lit a bonfire and used their searchlight to light up the nearby village as everyone celebrated the victory.

They were eventually sent down to Marchwood, Southampton, to a disused gun site while the War Office decided their future. Eventually, they were split up and sent to work in different places until they received their demob papers. Dot and a few other women from her unit were posted to Nottingham, to the Army Post Office, where she spent three months sorting mail and hating every moment of it. She was so used to being outside all day that being stuck inside, doing mundane work, was a kind of torture.

In February 1946, she was finally demobbed.

By the time they parted, all the girls on her site had signed each other's autograph books.

"Remember me in happy days at Barton. (Ruby 28/9/43)"

"Make new friends but keep the old. One is silver, one is gold. Brows may wrinkle, hair grows grey. But friendship never knows decay."

"Life is mostly froth and bubbles, two things stand like stone. Kindness in another's trouble, courage in your own. Hoping to see you as youthful as ever at our reunion in 1950."

"When the golden sun is setting and your mind from cares is free. When you sit and think of others, will you sometimes think of me?"

"A box or two of chocolates, a yard or two of lace. Tickets for the opera, powder for her face. Heaps of admiration, A Johnny that will pay. That is the inspiration of the modern miss today. (Merle 19/6/44)"

"After this war is over, then miles from a searchlight site we'll be. Oh boy we will be in clover, as happy as a bumblebee. No more manning searchlights, miles away from anywhere. No

more staying out all night, gazing into the dark, cold air. Best of luck, Nancy. 1944."

Throughout the war, Dot had been young, single and free. She had happily lived on small army sites deep in the English countryside with all her girlfriends, fixing engines and manning the searchlights every night. She cycled through pretty country lanes into the local village to buy supplies, experienced the excitement of someone receiving a postal order from home. She felt joy when someone in the regiment bought a few nice treats to share after dinner. Of course, there was rationing and stuff was in short supply, but in these remote villages, there always seemed to be someone with a few eggs or some spare flour who was willing to bake a few little cakes for *"those brave Army girls who risk their lives every night to keep us safe in our beds."*

While at the sites, Dot went to the occasional dance at the village hall. She was able to get dressed up for a change, putting those horrid, scratchy, and very unflattering uniforms aside for an evening. She made eyes at the few handsome young men in the hall. They were mostly farm workers–men who were staying put to do their war effort–or occasionally, local lads home on leave from the trenches. These were young men with sad eyes, young men who had seen so much horror they would never choose to tell their families back home.

Of course, there had been the odd romance. During the war years, several of Dot's colleagues got engaged to boys they had met at the dances–some even ended up marrying them.

Dot was cautious. She didn't want to end up with a broken heart–or worse–having a baby and no husband. She guarded her heart carefully. For the whole four-year duration of *her* war, she never gave her heart away completely. She came close only once with a young soldier. He was an engineer called James, who came to their site occasionally to bring a new engine part or fix something that was "too tricky for the women to do on their own." Later on, she was so relieved that she had only kissed him rather than giving in to his sexual demands. She heard that he had been sent out to France and perished along with all the other young men in his unit—never to return to his homeland, buried forever in foreign soil.

Dot kept a diary, just in case anyone would ever be interested to read about her experiences. Of course, she was very careful not to include any information that might get into enemy hands. Plus, the red leather diary was small—only three inches in size—so she reckoned that any German who managed to get their hands on it would need jolly good eyesight to read the tiny writing.

"January 1943... War news seems much more encouraging."

"August 23rd 1943... All ACK-ACK leave cancelled until further notice."

"August 30th 1943... Asked officer about French correspondence course, always a useful asset."

"September 3rd 1943... Today is the fourth year of the war. What might the coming months hold in store for us?"

"September 4th 1943... Shopping in Luton. Came back to site early. This all night business makes one terribly tired."

"September 8th 1943... Tonight at 6pm, the capitulation of Italy was announced. A little nearer victory."

"November 14th 1943... Mobile library, got two books."

"November 25th 1943... Coming back from leave, met a very nice young fellow on the train. Also received a letter from a sailor pal of my brother!"

"December 8th 1943... Bad abscess in teeth. Swollen face. Army dentist removed all my front teeth!"

"December 30th 1943... Grand time with a visiting pianist and a film show this evening."

"December 31st 1943... Last day of the year. On all night guard. Captain Green visited the site and gave us a very entertaining lecture. The YWCA mobile canteen also came!"

On the 10th June 1944, Dot, along with some of her army pals, was confirmed at St. Paul's Cathedral by the bishop of London. How proud her ancestors–ordinary people who hailed from the East End–would have been to see their little girl in such splendid surroundings. She even received a little red bound copy of the book, *Helps to Worship–Epistles & Gospels*, which was one she was to treasure all her life. Dot and her friends were thrilled; it was a real honour to be confirmed, but they also wondered if it was just another way of keeping up morale. Everyone was getting so terribly fed up with the war.

Dot took her responsibilities at the searchlight site very seriously.

In much the same way she had learnt to become an excellent tailoress, she was determined to become an expert on searchlights. She listened avidly during every lecture, learning about all the different mechanisms involved in the systems and how to ensure they were maintained properly. She took copious notes about everything in her little notebook, a flimsy cream paper booklet that read: *Supplied for the Public Service. S.O. Book 13.*

"Adjust and check B & C to get brightness to maximum. To give the clearest definition of a spot, or brightness. Aiming at strobing at single static break. Identification of target, range, and bearing."

There were charts, tasks and lists. In large letters at the back of the book, Dot had written: *TEST AND PREPARE FOR ACTION.*

She continued using her little diaries whenever she could. Sometimes there were long gaps in her entries, usually when there was a lot of enemy aircraft overhead. In these instances, she had to stay up all night manning the searchlights and didn't have time to write.

"January 1st 1945... Today begins another year. I am looking forward, as I know everyone is, to a brighter and victorious future. This evening, we wrote letters home and listened to records and the radio. A peaceful night for once."

"January 11th 1945... Snow still deep. During P.T. period this afternoon, we rigged up a toboggan and had some fun on a nearby slope. Thank goodness no officers arrived! Snowed again this evening."

"January 18th 1945... Warsaw was liberated after 5 years of German occupation. We had to sleep on the floor tonight, as all the bedding is already packed along with everything else on lorries, as we are moving sites tomorrow."

"January 19th 1945... Up at 4am, ready to move. Long journey, but the new site is not too bad."

"January 23rd 1945... More snow. Colder than ever, there appears to be no end to the snow this year. Had a couple of days leave, so met Aunty Rose and went to the Savoy Theatre, then dinner at the Strand Corner House. Very enjoyable evening".

"January 29ᵗʰ 1945... At last, the snow is beginning to thaw! Now the workmen have mended the windows, etc., at last, we have a chance to get the place shipshape. This site is nothing like as cosy as our last one."

"February 1ˢᵗ 1945... Now that the snow has cleared, you can really get a good idea of the Kentish countryside. This is quite a pretty little spot. If it stays fine, I might cycle into Sevenoaks tomorrow to do a bit of shopping and buy a new book."

"March 26ᵗʰ 1945... Called on duty most of the night. Engaged quite a few hostile 'doodlebugs,' a change from the usual 'rockets.'

"April 1ˢᵗ 1945... News good – Allies well beyond the Rhine – wonder how much longer!!! No night ops here owing to weather. The countryside is beginning to look very beautiful. The woods next to our site have masses of violets with the most heavenly scent. Also primrose and wood anemones. 'Oh to be in England, now that April's here.'"

"April 12ᵗʰ 1945... Hottest day this year so far. Painted the equipment. On night guard duty. Bullseye tonight."

"April 19ᵗʰ 1945... As the Allied armies are advancing into Germany, they are finding concentration camps with millions of slave workers. The world is finally hearing the truth about the appalling atrocities that have taken place. Things that are so unspeakable, so hard to be believed of a civilised world. Never until this moment have I felt such hatred of another race. What hope can there possibly be for world peace when such bestial, in-human actions seem to have been condoned by a whole country?"

"April 23ʳᵈ 1945... Miss Drayton and her local amateur dramatic society came to site and put on a very good show.

Tomorrow we are looking forward to a grand day out at our troop sports day at the Orpington Sports Ground."

"April 24th 1945... Today marks 3 years in the ATS. I have very often been very fed up during this time, but I certainly never regret joining up. Here there is a companionship which is hard to find in civvy street. One meets so many different types of people and gains altogether a wider view of the world.

Berlin is now two thirds in the hands of the Allies and great headway is being made against the Japs in Burma. Maybe this damn war is coming to an end at last."

"May 8th 1945... The day before my 24th birthday and we have won the war! Germany has unconditionally surrendered to the Allies. Celebrations are erupting all around the world. Maybe now we can all get home to our families and try to start repairing the harm this dreadful war has caused. My heart bleeds for all the people across the world who have lost loved ones. Hopefully their sacrifices will not be in vain, and a destructive war like this will never happen again."

1946–BACK TO CIVVY STREET

On the 18th October 1949, four years after the end of the war, Dot received a letter from the War Office, inviting her to apply for her war medals. Those wonderful years–years when she had been so happy–were behind her. Distant, happy memories, despite all the sadness the war had brought to the world.

Going back to civvy street was hard for Dot. She had grown so used to the camaraderie on the searchlight sites, where all the women had relied on each other for company, food, and their collective safety. Although it had been hard and rather dangerous work, it had also been exhilarating. Going back home to London, to a bombed city where rubble from destroyed buildings was everywhere she looked, was rather daunting.

She missed the quiet of the countryside, the kindness of the locals, cycling down pretty country lanes, the wind blowing in her hair, and the heady smell of the violets and bluebells in the woods near their camp. They had moved camps a few times over the years, going wherever the need for searchlights was greatest.

Dot had been so proud to have joined the 93rd Searchlight Regiment of the Royal Artillery–an all-female air defence unit, set up in September 1942. She had begun her training six months earlier; there had been so much to learn about the machinery and the operation of the searchlights themselves. It had been quite a contrast to sitting in the little tailor's rooms in Soho.

She had spent time at camps near Hatfield in Hertfordshire, Gaddesden, and Sevenoaks, but especially loved their camp at Barton-le-Clay in Bedfordshire.

She looked down at the navy blue jacket on her lap. She was hand-stitching the lining into it and the expensive silky fabric made her think of the uniform she had been issued when she joined the army. Of course, that uniform had been nothing like the stuff she was sewing now, but although her army uniform had been a rather boring and unflattering khaki colour, it had been made of good quality fabric. She smiled as she remembered the list of clothing she had been given on admission to the ATS in 1941. It was exactly the same uniform that young Princess Elizabeth, later to become the Queen of England, had worn when she too became an ATS girl. They had all been so proud to be serving their country alongside her.

Dot remembered when she had been given her army number and **Soldier's Service and Pay Book,** a small brown leather book that stated: *"You will always carry this book on your person. You must produce this book whenever called upon to do so by a competent military authority, viz, Officer, Warrant Officer, N.C.O. or Military Policeman."*

Issued to ATS PERSONNEL

<u>Clothing:</u>

One greatcoat (size small).
One cape. Anti-gas.
One wallet. Anti-gas.
One ATS cap (size small).
One serge ATS jacket (size small).
One pair canvas shoes (size 5).
Two pairs brown ATS shoes (size 5).
One ATS skirt (size 2).
One badge cap.
One kit bag (universal).
Two belts, ATS corsets (size 2).
Three brassieres (size 2).
One identity disk with cord set.
One field dressing.
One fork.
One pair knitted gloves.
One housewife (small sewing kit).
One pullover jersey.
Three pairs ATS knickers (size small).
One table knife.
One spare pair of laces.
Four ATS shirts (size 2).
Eight collars (size 2).
Two pairs of pyjamas (size small).
Four pairs of ATS stockings (size 2).

Three ATS ties.
Two hand towels.
Three ATS vests (size medium).

Equipment:

Four ear protectors.
One water bottle.
One steel helmet.
One ground sheet.
One camouflage net.
One drinking mug.

One anti-gas respirator set:

Container, facepiece, haversack.
Anti-dimming outfit.
Anti-gas ointment.
Waste cotton.
Six eyeshields.

Cleaning and Toilet Articles:

One brass cleaner.
One brass button brush.
One ATS hairbrush.
One shoe polishing brush.
One toothbrush.
One hair comb.

As well as her personal details, the little brown book listed all the training and exams she would eventually pass and the vaccinations she received, and there was even a section at the back where she could make a will. That page read: "*Solely for use on active service. This Will page must not be used until you have been placed under orders for Active Service. On completion to be despatched to the officer in charge of records by O.C. Unit.*"

The bit about the will had made Dot a bit nervous when she began. Suddenly, she had realised she was in a pretty dangerous position and acknowledged that the Army wanted to be prepared in case she was killed on duty.

But of course, she hadn't died. However, she did know of women on other sites who had been killed. She just guessed that God had other plans for her. Otherwise, why would she have been saved when so many others had lost their lives in that senseless war?

On the 1ˢᵗ February 1946, she went to the Military Dispersal Unit at Guildford to return her army greatcoat. She had followed the instructions in her ATS Release book to the letter.

"*If you are returning your greatcoat to any railway station or to a unit notified, this page (which will be extracted by the Railway Company or a Unit) must be presented intact in this book with your greatcoat before the expiration of your Release leave, as shown on AFX 202D. The greatcoat should be neatly folded and tied with strong string.*"

And then, she returned to her old life.

It had been hard going back to the tailoring rooms in Soho. All the old Jewish tailors looked so much older; the war had been so hard on them. So many were grieving for family members and friends lost, so many poor souls had perished in the concentration camps.

But one thing was for sure–they were delighted to have their little Dot back.

"Oh my, how we have missed you, our little angel. Now you are a fine young woman–strong and so brave. Any man would be lucky to have you as his wife!"

Dot settled back in after some time. She enjoyed the sewing, but missed the searchlights. Every day at lunchtime, she popped out to Berwick Street Market, bought an apple, and sat on a bench watching the world go by. Now, after the sad and grey war years, there was great excitement. Princess Elizabeth had announced that she was going to marry Philip Mountbatten and Dot's little sewing room (on behalf of Gieves of Old Bond Street) was going to make Philip's wedding outfit. As a serving naval officer, he would be in full uniform.

Dot was so proud to tell her friends that she was helping to sew the wedding suit for the future queen's husband.

NEW LOVE

I t was Boxing Day 1948, and Dot had been home from war for a couple of years.

She was glad that the war was over at last, that Hitler and his gang of vicious thugs were all dead, defeated, or as some believed, hiding in remote parts of Europe or South America. At the same time, part of her missed it all–the excitement, the fear of never knowing what the next day would bring, the camaraderie of her army pals. She missed the searchlight sites in the remote countryside. She missed the quietness, the darkness, the sounds and smells of country life. There, when she was alone, watching the dark skies for enemy aircraft, she was able to think, to make plans for what she would do with her life when the war was over. She had written in her diary... *"Once Hitler is defeated, my proper life will begin. I will travel the world, have adventures, paint, and write. My life will be glorious."*

Of course, she was happy to be back home and in the loving arms of her dad and brother, but London was so noisy in comparison to the countryside.

Still, there was plenty of time. She was young, only 26.

For now, while she was saving to travel the world, she was content.

She had gone back to the little tailor's room in Soho and all the men had welcomed her with open arms. They had never expected to see their little apprentice again.

In her spare time, Dot loved to go dancing, to the pictures, or to the theatre. Sometimes she went with her old school friend Rosie, sometimes with Lily Cloke, a friend from her Battersea days.

She had known Lily since she was nine years old, since they had moved to Battersea with her step-mother. The Cloke family had been great friends of Lizzie's family, but of course, after Dot's move to Morden, Lizzie's abandonment, and then her sudden death, the two families had drifted apart.

One day in 1937, quite by chance, the two girls had bumped into each other at Victoria Station. The years seemed to have slipped away as they chatted and since then, they had been inseparable. They had even signed up to join the ATS together and posed for a street photographer on Regent Street in their smart new uniforms.

Unfortunately, the war had divided them physically. They each went off to their separate units on different sites, but whenever they were both home on leave, they always met up. The two girls usually had tea and toasted teacakes at a Lyons Corner House.

Now that the war was over, Dot and Lily were single and carefree, both holding down good jobs and happy to spend their precious evenings and weekends enjoying themselves.

Dot would often rush home from work, realise her best dress still wasn't quite dry, and have to iron it with the heavy flat iron on the old kitchen table so that it would be ready to wear dancing that evening. Sometimes it was even still a wee bit damp when she put it on. If only she could afford more than one decent dress! But of course, she was saving up to go travelling, to see the world.

She spent a quiet Christmas Day at home with her dad in 1948. Her brother John had been with them for a couple of hours in the morning and had given them each a small present wrapped in bright paper—the very same wrapping paper that Dot had bought and hidden under her bed. Still, she didn't care that he had obviously crept into her room and borrowed it; at least he had remembered to buy them a present!

For his dad, John had wrapped a few packets of Senior Service cigarettes and a box of matches. For Dot, he had found a pretty little green glass box with a lid.

"Hope you like it, Sis. Bertha thought it would be good for your dressing table, and I know green is your favourite colour."

Dot did like it; in fact, she was thrilled with it. Who cared if that awful Bertha, John's latest girlfriend, had chosen it? It was still quite beautiful, and what he said was true. She did love anything green. Many of her happiest memories involved green things: the old green eiderdown she had slept under as a child at Camden Town, the lovely apple green silk dress her step-mother had made especially for her, and her current best dress, a lovely creation made of green crepe.

John had had so many girlfriends since being discharged from the Royal Navy. All the women seemed to chase after her tall, handsome brother. Some of them had been nice, sweet girls, whilst others, like Bertha, left something to be desired in Dot's eyes. They were all young and beautiful and hung onto his every word as he recounted tales of his years at sea. To give him some credit, he *had* been on many dangerous missions, but listening to him speak while he was trying to impress his latest loves would have one thinking he single-handedly won the war!

After John left that Christmas morning, Dot and her dad had a quiet rest of the day. They were happy just to be together at last; their distance during the war years had taken a toll on everyone.

On Boxing Day morning, they walked to the Tube station together.

Valentine hugged Dot as if he would never let her go. She was so precious to him.

"Have a nice time at Lily's, love. Don't forget to give them all my regards, especially old Mr. Cloke. Can't believe he's getting on for a hundred! See you at Rose's on Tuesday. They can't wait to see you, so try not to be too late getting there. I know how you and Lily chatter on."

Dot left her dad on the train, as he was going on to Edgware, to stay at the house Rose and Cyril bought there in 1945. He had been a bit worried about how they would cope moving out there. Rose and his mum (who had gone with them) were such city girls; they had been born and bred in the East End within the sound of the Bow Bells—Edgware was so different from Camden Town. Much to his surprise though, they were thriving, and had taken to it like ducks to water.

As they hugged on parting, neither Dot nor Valentine had any idea that the events of that day would change the entire course of Dot's life.

It was always noisy at the Clokes' house, which was a little terraced house in Battersea, just around the corner from where Dot had lived as a child and had gone to Sleaford Street School.

Dot smiled to herself as she walked the streets from the Tube station. Nothing had really changed. There were a lot of bomb-damaged houses around, still piles of rubble everywhere, but the essence of the place was still the same.

"Hello, my girl. Come in, come in. It's bloomin' freezing out there, don't want all that cold air coming into the parlour. Mind you, it's pretty hot in here, what with all these bodies. And now our Edgar is threatening to start playing the piano so we can all have a sing-song."

Dot smiled at the little woman and gave her a big hug. She loved Lily's mum; in fact, she loved the whole Cloke family–that loud, noisy, nosy, and loving bunch.

Lily got up from where she had been sitting on the uncomfortable looking sofa.

"Thank Gawd you're here, Dot. I've been stuck sitting on that horrid sofa, talking to Aunty Mildred for hours. I wouldn't mind if she had much to say, but all she seems to talk about is how dreadful it is that some of the local girls had flings with the Yanks who were stationed here. I told her that I admired the ones who were brave enough to become war brides and take off for a new life in America. Mind you, I do feel awfully sad for the ones that got left behind, pregnant and abandoned. They've had

to pay a high price for their chocolate and a few silk stockings! At least now you're here, I can have some decent conversation."

The promised sing-song started almost as soon as Dot sat down. Lily's younger brother, Edgar, was something of a frustrated music hall entertainer, so he would find any excuse to sit down at the piano and rattle out some of the old favourites.

Dot was a bit shy, so it took her a while to relax and join in with the raucous singing. One song after another.

"You'll find us all, doing the Lambeth Walk."

"And a nightingale sang in Berkeley Square."

"Maybe it's because I'm a Londoner, that I love London Town."

"They'll be bluebirds over the White Cliffs of Dover."

That last one made them all a bit teary eyed. After all, the war had only been over for a few years and England was still recovering from the devastation.

Dot looked across the room and smiled shyly at the handsome young man who was staring at her. Lily noticed.

"Ooh Dot, shall I introduce you? That's Edgar's new friend. They met at the cycling club. He's very handsome, isn't he?"

"Hey Edgar, be a gent and introduce your new friend."

"Oh sorry, Dot. This is Ben. He's joined my cycling club. Used to be in the Air Force like me, but the lucky bugger spent the war years sunning himself in South Africa."

The young man in question smiled.

"Yes, I'm afraid I'm guilty on both counts. I was in Africa for the whole war and I have joined the cycle club. You two could join too if you like, they're happy to have lady members."

Lily snorted.

"Can you really see me balancing on a bike, Ben? It would have to be a very sturdy one to take my weight. But Dot's good on a bike, she used one all the time when she was stuck miles from civilization on those searchlight sites. Didn't you, Dot?"

Dot smiled weakly. She was having trouble concentrating. He was so handsome and such a gentleman. It had been a long time since she had met someone who made her heart flutter.

BEN'S STORY

Ben was born in Peabody Buildings in Southwark, South London. Until he was eleven years old, he lived in those same tenement buildings, surrounded by his extended family–grandparents, great grandparents, aunties, uncles, and cousins. It was a marvelous place for a little boy to grow up. They didn't have very much money, but Ben grew up surrounded by so much love.

They were ordinary Londoners, Cockney and proud. His family had lived in Southwark for generations and all of his ancestors were buried in the old church graveyard by the river.

The River Thames–Ben's playground.

He loved to wander through the little cobbled alleyways leading down to the river. He would spend hours watching the big ships–laden with cargo–come into the docks. His dad, Eustace, worked at Surrey Commercial Docks; most of the other men in his family either worked there, or on the river, as ferrymen, fishermen, or lightermen.

Then there was Ben's Great Granny Mabel, along with the other ladies who worked at Borough Market selling fish. He found it amazing to think that Mabel, such a sweet old lady, had been working on the very same stall since she was a little girl, back in 1840!

Little Ben knew almost everyone. He was such a sunny, happy child, always willing to stop and chat to anybody. Not to mention, he was smart. Despite being a child from the slums, everyone knew he was different, that he had a good brain, that with the right encouragement, he would go far in life.

His parents adored him. His mum, Lou, had lost four babies before he was born. She had been heartbroken–so heartbroken that she had vowed never to have another baby, never to go through that awful loss and pain again. But her husband Eustace had persuaded her that it wouldn't happen again, that "next time" all would be well. Eventually, she gave in and her son, her precious Ben, was born in 1922–four years after the end of World War One. That had been such a dreadful time, so many young men lost, so many families bereft. Once it was over, they had to try and look toward the future, to hope for a better world after so much sacrifice.

Lou turned out to be a wonderful mother, utterly devoted to her boy and his well-being. It made Eustace very happy to see them together, his beloved wife and son.

Little Ben flourished. It would have been hard not to, he was constantly surrounded by so many wonderful people who loved him. When he wasn't wandering along beside the river, pestering his aunties at their fish stall in the market, or at home eating the delicious meals his mum cooked, he could be found playing with his mates outside in the yard. The yard was a huge concrete area surrounded on all four sides by the old brick tenements that made up Peabody Buildings. In the middle were the communal washing lines, handily placed near the big laundry room, which every flat in the buildings shared. There were communal toilets too, shared between several families. No one had their own bathroom in the flats, but there was a communal bathhouse in each building and most people were happy to use that.

Lou was one who didn't like the shared facilities; she longed for a bathroom of her very own. Most Sunday evenings she would boil up kettles of hot water and fill up the old tin bath. Once soaking in the bath, which was placed in front of the fire, she would luxuriate in there for at least half an hour.

"Oh come on, Eustace. If you really loved me you wouldn't moan about having to keep adding hot water. And at least you know you'll get the benefit of it soon."

She was always the first to use the bath, followed by little Ben, then finally Eustace. Occasionally, he would grumble.

"Why do I always have to go last? The water is always grubby by the time I get in. Maybe we should change the order sometimes and I could go first?"

She would laugh at the disgruntled look on his face.

"For Gawd's sake. I don't want to get in that water after you've been in there. Heavens only knows what grubby germs you might bring back from those docks! And anyway, a lady should never have to be last at anything. You remember that Ben, my lad. When you eventually get yourself married and have a nice wife, you must always treat her like a queen. Who knows? By the time that happens, you might even be lucky enough to have a house with an inside bathroom! Don't s'pose I'll ever see that

for myself, but you just might. You're smart enough to get a good job that pays decent money."

Lou wasn't having a dig at her husband by saying this. Sheand Eustace had both grown up in Peabody Buildings, so knew no other life. However, Eustace had been at sea for seven years, and they both realised that not everyone in the world lived as poorly as they did. Some people had much worse lives too; Eustace had been shocked to see the poverty in India and other parts of the world during his travels.

When Ben was four years old, he was joined by a little brother.

Baby Dennis was born with a shock of blonde–almost white–curls, which was quite different from Ben, who had a head of thick, straight, dark hair.

The two young brothers thrived, until the dark, dreadful day when little Dennis was struck down with the dreaded diphtheria, just two days after his second birthday.

If only they had been rich people, they could have afforded a doctor. Instead, they had dilly-dallied, worried about spending their last sixpence calling out the doctor. They just hoped and prayed that little Dennis would get better, despite knowing from bitter experience that too many infants died in the slums from a lack of money. They never in a million years thought it would happen to one of their own.

He was gone the very next day. The little boy died in his own bed, surrounded by his loving family. Everyone was shocked and heartbroken.

It took Lou a very long time to recover. She had lost babies before, but they had been miscarriages. They were babies who died before they had a chance to draw their first breath—to her, this was so much worse. To have given birth to a child, to have nurtured and loved him for two years, just to have him snatched away with almost no warning was more than she could bear. She went into a deep decline approaching madness—something she seemed to have no control over.

Everyone tried to help her, of course. They made sure she was never alone, in case her grief caused her to do something silly. They all knew that losing a child sometimes made women lose their minds completely. There had been several cases where women from Peabody Buildings, finding their grief too much to bear, had thrown themselves from the roof onto the hard concrete square below. Others had thrown themselves into the River Thames late at night, when there were few people around and the chances of being fished out of the cold water and rescued were slim. A couple of others had been declared insane and sent to the local asylum.

Lou was luckier than those women. She had a big, loving family that ensured no such harm came to her. They watched over her day and night. Slowly, after several months of constant weeping, she began to come back to life, bit by bit.

"Dad, why does Mum cry all the time?"

Eustace put his arm around the little boy. He was too choked up to speak for a moment or two.

"Oh Ben, she's just sad about losing our Dennis. She loved your little brother so much. We all did."

"I loved him too, Dad. I was going to start teaching him things like how to count to twenty, roll marbles, and play hopscotch. Now he's gone. Will you get me another little brother?"

Eustace looked down at his eldest son. Now, his only son. He patted the boy's head gently.

"I don't know, son. You can't just replace people, especially lovely ones like our Dennis."

Eustace's heart was breaking too. He had loved both his boys equally, but he knew that Lou had had a soft spot for their youngest one. Now he was in Heaven and Lou was in utter despair.

"Did Mum like our Dennis better than me?" The little boy's voice was rather forlorn.

"Course not, lad. You're both our special precious boys and of course we love you the same."

Eustace was aware that he was using the present tense by saying *"love,"* rather than *loved.*

"But I heard Mum telling Granny Jane that he was her golden boy, the best of us. And that no-one would ever take his place in her heart."

"Oh, Ben. She didn't mean that she loved him more than you. It's just that sometimes, when you lose people you love, you want to remember them always, remember how very special they were. That's what your mum was talking about. Just her way of remembering our little Dennis."

There were no more children after that. Lou knew that she had been in a very dark place and didn't want to put herself through any more heartache or sorrow. She kept Dennis's black-edged burial card, together with her favourite photo of him, propped up on the mantelpiece.

Ben grew used to the idea of being an only child. His cousin, Arthur, who lived in the room next door with his widowed mum, Ann, and their two grannies, Mabel and Ann, was an only child too, so the two boys became bosom pals and spent most of their free time together. Arthur was older than Ben, a gentle, quiet boy who had lost his dad in the war. Together they explored Southwark–their Southwark. Sometimes they'd go with their Grandad Arthur, sometimes they'd adventure on their own. They loved to go mudlarking, digging in the muddy banks of the Thames for treasures. Sometimes they found money–old Victorian pennies mostly– and once they had uncovered a Roman coin, which was very exciting. They dug up lots of old clay pipes and broken bits of porcelain, but they always hoped to find some real treasure one day. Surely, with all the big boats coming from exotic places around the world, they would definitely stumble across something really valuable. They always took their treasures home, still covered in smelly, filthy mud. Much to their mums' horror, they insisted on cleaning their prizes and displaying them on the mantelpiece in their bedrooms.

Both the boys were very smart. Although they only attended the small, dilapidated old school around the corner on Southwark Street, their teachers recognised they both had good brains and that, given the right encouragement, they could achieve more than the average boy from the slums. For those boys, the only expectation would be to work on the river, in the docks, or at the market, just as generations of their families had done before them.

Both Ben and Arthur loved their Aunty Astrid, their mums' older sister.

Ben's mum had five sisters, all older and much taller than she was. His mum was a little titch, standing less than five feet tall in her stockinged feet, and her sisters towered over her. It was no wonder she had always felt a bit small and shy around them. They all loved her dearly, of course, their baby sister Lou, but they did have a way of making her feel less important than them. Whenever she complained about it, their mum always said it was just "how it was," that she should think herself lucky she had any sisters at all.

Ben loved all his aunties of course, but Aunty Astrid was definitely his favourite.

She seemed so exotic and exciting, a bit different from all the others. She wasn't married with children like the rest of them, in fact, he had often heard his mum say that she was *"married to those books of hers, instead."*

It was true that Aunty Astrid loved books. She worked in a posh bookshop in the city, and in her spare time, she was planning to be a famous author. She lived in Chelsea, but every time she came back to Southwark to visit Peabody Buildings, she bought a pile of books with her as gifts—romantic novels for her sisters and adventure stories for the two boys.

"It is very important that you boys read books. How else are you going to learn all about the world? Reading got me to where I am today, broadened my horizons, made me realise that the world is a big, exciting place. I don't want you two just settling for Southwark all your life. Get out there and explore the world. Make the most of your lives."

The rest of the family would raise their eyebrows when Astrid talked like this. Most of them were quite happy with their lot—they liked living in Peabody Buildings by the river in Southwark, where generations of their family had lived before them. Although having a bit more money would be nice, they were mostly content walking the very same streets all their ancestors had... except soppy old Astrid.

Ben, like most children in his situation who were growing up in a happy home, didn't realise he came from a poor background. Until he was eleven and started at the "big school," he just assumed that everyone lived as his family did—from one payday to another. Every Friday, he would rush to the docks to meet Eustace from work so that he might be able to persuade him to buy a few sweets from the old tobacconist shop on the corner before disappearing into the pub with his mates. Ben was used to the rather grubby, cobbled streets of Southwark— the smells and sounds that wafted from the river and the pubs late at night. He knew that often, people would get sick and die in Peabody Buildings just because they couldn't afford to pay for a doctor. After all, that had happened to Dennis, his own little brother. He was sad about all the beggars on the street corners—holding out their dirty hands for a few pennies—and he always smiled at them as he walked past. It really upset him when they were young, some obviously orphaned and as young as seven or eight years old, with no home to go to. He often saw them sneak into the market just before it closed to scrounge some stale bread or rotten fruit. Some of the market traders would take pity on them and give them an old sack or newspaper so they could sleep a bit more comfortably on the cold pavement.

Then there were all the young girls with their babies, thrown onto the streets because their families were ashamed that they got pregnant before they were married. Some of them were only thirteen or fourteen. They had been treated roughly, sometimes by boys or men they had imagined themselves in love with, who had promised them the earth but disappeared as soon as they learnt of the coming baby. Some were ex-housemaids who had worked in big mansions and been preyed on by their masters or his sons, then summarily sacked as soon as their bellies started to swell. Others were the result of incest; living in such cramped conditions often meant that fathers, uncles, cousins, and even brothers were tempted by girls' nubile beauty and innocence. They, too, were abandoned once the evidence of the man's crime started to show.

These young mothers got sadder and thinner the longer they slept on the streets, and often their poor, malnourished babies died in their arms. A few women turned to prostitution just to feed themselves. They often died before they turned thirty, from dreadful venereal diseases inflicted on them by their clients at the docks—sailors, dockers, merchants, and a few rich men who sought their fun from poor, vulnerable women. None of them cared in the slightest to hear of another girl dropping dead; there were always so many more waiting in the wings to take their places. The men could satisfy their desires and walk away; the women were left to pay the price. And of course, all of society, even some women's neighbours in the slums of South London, looked the other way.

"Well, she was always a bit of a flighty one."

"Not surprised her family kicked her out, she's no better than she should be."

"Always knew she was a wrong 'un."

"No wonder she got herself in the family way, did you see the way she used to eye up the boys in church?"

"It's the babies I feel sorry for. They didn't ask to be born."

Somehow, the poor young women were always made out to be the villains of the piece. There was rarely a word of criticism about the men who had impregnated them.

"After all, boys will be boys. What did she expect if she made eyes at him like that?"

"Her dresses were always too short, I often caught sight of her ankles."

"That family has always been a bit loose in their behaviour. That's the second daughter of theirs to get pregnant before she was thirteen. Disgusting, I call it."

"Of course, young men will always need to sow their oats. It's happened for hundreds of years. These girls just need to behave more decently."

Sometimes Ben would talk to his mum about it. Her heart would break as she listened to him. He was such a sweet, kind, and caring boy. He was going to have a hard passage in life; he cared about people too much.

Just before his 11th birthday, Ben's mum and dad announced that they were moving. They were leaving Peabody Buildings and Southwark altogether, going miles away out to the country, to a place called Rose Hill.

Ben was upset at first. He was worried about leaving everything and everyone he had ever known. His mum said it would be good, "a real adventure," but he wasn't so sure. He didn't think his dad was too sure, either; his mum seemed to be the only one who was really excited about the move.

"Oh come on, love, don't look so glum. You'll love it once you've settled in! There'll be lots of space for you to kick your football around, and I bet you'll make lots of new friends in no time."

"But what about my school? I like it there."

"Don't be silly, love. You'd have to leave there next year anyway, and the new one looks really nice. Quite posh, nice smart uniform, and what about that cricket pitch? I reckon you're going to be very happy at the grammar school. You'll be able to learn French and maybe even Latin. Just look how well our Arthur's done since they moved to Whitstable."

It was true. Ben's cousin Arthur, his lifelong playmate and confidante, now lived in Whitstable, an old seaside town in Kent.

Arthur's mum, Ann, had remarried. Now she, her new husband, Arthur, and Ann and Lou's mother, Jane, lived down there.

Young Arthur had found the move hard at first. He missed everyone at Peabody Buildings, he missed everything about London. But then, he was lucky enough at the tender age of 15 to get an apprenticeship with a local boatbuilder. He soon realised that he loved living by the sea and working with his hands. In no time at all, the rather pale, weakly boy from the slums gained weight, developed some muscles and a suntan, and was content.

"And another thing, Ben. In the new house, we'll have a garden where you and your dad can grow things. But most exciting of all, we'll have our very own bathroom... and an inside toilet!"

Sometimes Ben thought that was all his mum wanted–her own bathroom and inside toilet. He had never been able to understand why she fussed so much about using the shared facilities in the Buildings. He didn't care if he had to queue for ages to use the lavatory, and he quite liked using the communal bathhouse. Although of course, he also wouldn't really have cared if he never had a bath again. He would have been quite happy just washing his body under the outside tap in the concrete yard.

Eventually, they all settled into their new house with its garden, bathroom, and luxurious inside toilet. No more bedpans under the beds for them!

Ben settled happily into his new school–*Sutton Grammar School for Boys*. He made new friends and loved his lessons, joined the local Boys' Brigade, and proudly wore the smart uniform once a month at church parades. He played football on the large, open spaces behind the house with all his new mates, and sometimes helped his dad plant vegetables in their little garden. Eustace had become something of an avid gardener since the move. It was such a change from being stuck working on the docks all day or cooped up in their crowded little rooms in Peabody Buildings. Here, in his new garden, he could daydream as he tended his plants. He grew cabbages, kale, potatoes, and tomatoes. One side of the long, narrow garden was divided into two–the top half was where he grew flowers for Lou. He just loved to see her face light up when he cut her a bunch of asters, dahlias, daffodils, sweet peas, or gladioli. She would hug him and rush to fill her favourite vase with water. The vase, which always sat in pride of place on the mantelpiece, had belonged to her Granny Mabel, and Eustace remembered how it had always been her dream to have it constantly full of pretty blooms. He planned his flower garden to ensure that there was always something available. Making his wife and his boy happy had always been the most important thing in his life. Of course, for now, he still trudged up to town every day. He couldn't see himself being able to retire until he was at least 60. Eustace wasn't sure if his aging old body would cope with the hard labour of being a docker for many more years, but at least these days, he could hop on the Tube at London Bridge after work knowing he was going back to his little sanctuary in the country. Although Rose Hill was only a few miles away from Southwark as the crow flies, it might as well have been in another country with all the contrasts. When he was fed up digging his garden, Eustace could wander up to the local shops and chat to the old man in the tobacconist's, the lady at the greengrocer's, and old Bert at the baker's. He could even pop into the Rose and Crown for a quick pint if he wanted to (and had enough spare pennies!). His Lou and little Ben loved the cinema, so sometimes they all went along to the Gaumont to watch a film. If they were feeling really flush, they would treat themselves to a bag of chips to eat on the way home.

The years passed quickly. Ben thrived; he excelled at school and made some great mates. It became obvious that with his quick brain, he was not destined to spend his life doing mundane work like his parents did. Although he could see that they were both content enough with their lot, he had bigger ambitions. He was not going to waste his life lugging heavy crates around on the docks or toiling away in some boring old factory like his mum did.

Instead, he left school at age 15 and went straight to the technical college, where he studied advanced maths and electrical engineering. It was marvelous; he learnt something new every day and would come home quoting facts and figures about things his parents had never heard of and didn't really understand. They were immensely proud of him for his academic achievements.

He was about to sit for final exams when Adolf Hitler invaded Poland.

Ben and his best friend, Sid, were excited to join up—to fight for King and Country and protect England from invasion.

They didn't tell their parents beforehand, of course. They just knew that Ben's mum and dad, as well as Sid's mum, would try to talk them out of it.

They were both accepted into the Royal Air Force, but after scraping through his medical examinations, Ben was told he could not be the fighter pilot he had planned and dreamt to be. Instead, he would work on aircraft maintenance. Sid passed all the tests with flying colours and was accepted into the pilot training scheme. It was a short, hurried training course for bright-eyed, innocent young men, many of whom, like Sid, were still teenagers. The course proved to offer no protection when Sid's plane was shot down just a few weeks later by enemy fire. All the crew perished.

Ben was mortified, heartbroken to hear about the death of his best friend. Somehow, it was made even worse by the fact that, so far, he was having a rather cushy war. He was a classic *Brylcreem Boy*, as the handsome young men of the RAF became known. He was posted out to various sites in South Africa and had spent his war years enjoying the sunshine and new, exciting scenery of Johannesburg, Cape Town, and East London. That last one always made him smile; East London, South Africa was nothing like the East London he knew and loved so well–the place he had left behind in Old Blighty.

Of course it wasn't all sunshine, pineapples, and curry. There was a dark side, too. Ben and his mates mourned all their friends, the boys who had flown off one day on a mission, never to return. Lost forever in a foreign land–no bodies for their mothers to bury or grieve over, just a cold, stark telegram. *"We regret to inform you. Lost in action."* From 1939 to 1945, all over the world, families received this sad news. It was news that would change family dynamics forever.

Ben, along with many of his colleagues, suffered mentally. They were so young, so full of hope and enthusiasm, so certain they were helping to make the world a safer, happier place. They obeyed their superiors, even when they had doubts. Surely the big-wigs knew what they were doing, right? Surely they wouldn't just keep sending all these bright young men to their deaths?

Facing daily anxiety and the relentless loss of their mates– young men like themselves, just boys really–they began to question the sense of fixing the damaged planes. For what? So they could go on another mission, another night of danger?

It took its toll.

Ben, like others, felt his grip on common sense being stripped away. He asked the wrong questions of the wrong people and was sent away, not home to England on extended leave, but to a small clinic somewhere deep in the African countryside, where they treated airmen with *"anxiety."* After a brief stay there, he was sent back to keep the aircraft flying. After all, talented engineers such as himself were in short supply.

Ben's war was over by 1946, and he returned to England as a handsome, sun-tanned 23-year-old. A man changed. He had left as a naïve young 18-year-old, a boy barely out of school. In the five years he was away, he went from a kid who knew almost nothing of himself or the world to someone who had learnt so much. He had met so many great people, including people with a different colour skin from him, but who had the same hearts. It had changed his life forever, but after returning, he would rarely speak of it.

After the war, it took Ben a while to settle down, to get his equilibrium back. He had been away so long. During those long war years, he'd had barely any contact with anyone at home. There had been the odd letter, of course, but they had been so highly censored that it was often impossible to read them. All the black pen marks obliterated anything that might be considered a risk to the war effort. Ben had scoffed at that. What on earth could his mum's ramblings about tea shortages, her gossip about her sisters, and the stories of her new friends at the flower seed factory where she worked have to do with defeating the enemy? In his view, it was the women like his mum, tough, ordinary women, who were keeping the country afloat. Without them and their determination to keep everyone and everything they loved safe, lesser mortals would surely have caved into despair before the war was over.

It was hard going to visit Sid's mum on his return. Ben felt so guilty that he was still alive while his best friend had perished. That poor woman had so much to contend with; her other two sons had been fighting in France and returned home very damaged. Her only daughter, Sid's young sister, had fallen prey to an American airman and had given birth to his baby–his promises of taking her back to Texas with him as his war bride came to nothing when it transpired that he already had a wife and three children back home.

But of course, life went on.

Ben went back to the technical college, passed all his exams with flying colours, and managed to secure a job with Philips Electrical at Century House on Shaftesbury Avenue, in the Amplifier and Radio department. He had "made it"– working in the West End of London, wearing a smart tweed jacket, collar, and tie.

Although Eustace was very proud of him, he often teased his son: *"You come home looking just the same as when you left. Hardly a hair out of place. Don't know why your mum bothers to wash and iron you a clean shirt every day! Nothing ever gets dirty just sitting at that workbench of yours, while you make radios or whatever it is you do! You wouldn't last five minutes on the docks my lad, having to do real men's work!"*

Ben knew how lucky he was and he loved both his parents dearly. He was so grateful that they had both survived the war, that he had a loving home to come back to.

He joined the local cycling club and made lots of new friends. He loved the exhilaration of cycling, discovering new places, feeling the wind in his hair and the sun on his face. It reminded him of South Africa.

He was single for just three years after the war. He loved his single life because he had the best of both worlds—an adoring mother at home who took care of his every need and worshipped the ground he walked on, as well as a bevy of young beauties who did all they could to capture the attention of the handsome young man. Some of them had captured his attention for a while, but none of them truly captured his heart. That is, until he met Dot.

AFTER THE WEDDING

The loneliness was the hardest.

Just a few short years ago, Dot had been living with all the other ATS girls on the busy searchlight site. She sometimes wished for peace and seclusion on the sites, especially after yet another sleepless night manning the searchlights, constantly scanning the skies for signs of approaching enemy aircraft. It had been such an important job. Dangerous at times.

It was common knowledge amongst the ATS girls that several sites like theirs had received direct hits and suffered great loss of life. Many sites had been wiped out completely. The futures of many young women–women just like them– had been stolen by Hitler and his warmongering.

Of course, such tragedies were never made public–not until well after the war had ended. The powers that be, the shadowy men in suits at the top, thought it would be bad for public morale, bad for the general population to know of the losses. To them, it was much better to put on a brave face, to let people think that England and her brave men and women were indeed winning the war. If they knew the truth–the awful statistics of exactly how many brave young men and women had been lost–they had feared that the tide of opinion would turn. In the early years of the war, patriotism was at its highest; everyone believed they were fighting for a brave new world.

After her marriage to Ben, Dot had as much peace and seclusion as she wanted... and she hated it.

Since they had left Rosehill and moved to their new house in the country, she had been so unhappy.

Until that point, Dot had not realised what a townie she was. Apart from those few years during the war when she had lived in remote fields on the fringes of small, rural country villages, she had spent all her time in busy towns. She was born in London's Camden Town, sharing a house with most of her family–several generations all squished together and wrapped up in each other's lives. Then, she was in Battersea for a few years with her step-mum's big, noisy family.

They had moved to Morden when she was eleven, and although initially it had seemed quiet after London, she started working in the city when she was just 14. So all her life–until now–she had been used to the hustle and bustle, the noises, sounds, and smells of a crowded place.

Here, in this house, on this street, she felt adrift. Out of control.

Dot had initially been so excited when they were offered a council house.

Four years ago, after their wedding, Dot and Ben had moved in with her in-laws, Lou and Eustace. Dot would have much preferred that they had been able to have somewhere of their very own–even one room would have done–but the country was still recovering from the ravages of the war. There were bomb sites all over the city, whole streets of houses and buildings flattened to the ground. People were being housed wherever they could be, but there was a huge shortage of available properties.

"Come on, Squibs."

They had given each other that name on their honeymoon and she rather liked it. She had never had a nickname before… well, not unless you included those rather horrid ones when she was young: *"Second Hand Annie," "Dozy Dot,"* and then later, *"Clever Clogs."* She had been rather proud of that last one, reading and learning had always been her great passions.

"It'll be alright, I promise. My mum and dad don't mind us moving in with them. I know it'll be a bit of a squeeze, but at least we'll both be out at work all day. And Mum's not a bad cook; at least you won't have to worry about rushing home and getting my meal on the table every night! She's fed me well for all these years, she won't mind having another mouth to feed."

On their honeymoon, Ben had held her tightly in his arms as she sobbed–sobbed because she was happy to be married, yes, but also because she suddenly realised she would never go back to her own home again. Her brother's new wife had seen to that. Dot's new sister-in-law, Jean, had demanded that *she and John* move in with Valentine. She had even announced that as soon as Dot got married, they were planning to turn her bedroom into a nursery for the baby they were expecting, meaning she wouldn't even have a home to go back to for a weekend visit.

She sobbed about the loss of her mum and her step-mum. How lovely it would have been to have one of them at her wedding. She wished they had been there to help her plan everything–to help make her dress, to organise the catering for the party afterwards–but of course, they were both long dead.

She knew that her new sister-in-law didn't like her very much. She had even managed to steal the date Dot and Ben picked for their wedding: July 5th, 1949.

"Oh Dot, you wouldn't mind moving your wedding to another day, would you? Me and John really want a nice summer wedding and I had my heart set on July 5th."

Of course, Dot had acquiesced.

She loved her little brother and had always put his happiness before her own. Mind you, if she had known then that her new sister-in-law planned to evict her from her own home, it might have been a different story.

She had never really warmed to Jean. She wasn't sure if she was quite the right person to marry her lovely little brother. He'd had some wonderful girlfriends, girls Dot would have loved to have as a sister-in-law. Girls who would have been happy to share their new husband–and his home–with his loving sister.

Jean was older than John, a bit sharp-tongued, and rather judgemental. Dot sometimes wondered what on earth he saw in her.

A month or so after John and Jean's wedding, she realised why they had been in such a rush to get married. Jean stopped wearing her corset, and her swelling tummy was apparent.

So, Dot and Ben ended up having a March wedding instead. The ceremony was held at St. Lawrence's church, a lovely old stone building that had been standing in the same pretty graveyard for hundreds of years.

It happened on a sunny spring day. The daffodils were just peeping through the still-hard winter ground, and everyone was wearing thick coats over their wedding outfits as it was so chilly.

Dot had made her wedding dress herself, every last stitch done by hand. It was the most beautiful thing, made of watermarked satin, with a sweetheart neckline and tiny, satin-covered buttons all down the back and sleeves. Luckily, she had been saving up all her clothing coupons to buy the material, and she had even made her own veil. In her arms, she carried a huge bouquet of trailing carnations. Her two bridesmaids, little Barbara Cloke and Jean, carried enormous bouquets of tulips. She had only really wanted to have one bridesmaid, but Jean had insisted. Dot couldn't bring herself to say what she was really thinking, that Jean had not only stolen her first planned wedding day, but also her brother, her dad, and her childhood home. Since Jean had moved into the house in Morden, it somehow didn't feel like Dot's anymore. Even though she had still been living there 'til today–her wedding day–she knew Jean couldn't wait to get rid of her so she could be the only woman in the house. It seemed petty to say anything, so she just swallowed her anger and sewed a second bridesmaid dress, using more precious clothing coupons than she could really afford.

Dot was shaking a little as she walked slowly down the aisle of the little church, leaning rather heavily on her dad's arm for support. Shaking from the cold of March as well as the enormity of what she was about to do. Marrying Ben was going to change her life entirely. She would no longer be a free agent, able to come and go as she pleased. From now on, she was going to be beholden to that handsome man who was standing at the front, looking at her with such love and longing. She knew she loved him, of course she did, but was she really prepared to give up all her own hopes and dreams, just to be a good wife? Obviously, it was too late to back out now.

The strains of Mendelssohn's "Wedding March" filled the little church and Dot heard gasps from both sides of pews as she made her way towards Ben.

She knew it was her dress everyone was admiring. It was such a beautiful thing; she was really proud of her handiwork.

Her dress was simple, but elegant. Made of white satin, it had taken her months to sew, and she often stayed up late into the night working on it.

Lily Cloke watched Dot glide down the aisle. She was rather in awe of her friend's sewing talent. Of course, she had always known Dot was talented—you didn't get an apprenticeship with a big London tailor unless you were pretty good at sewing. Not to mention, you certainly didn't get welcomed back to the workshop with open arms after being away at war for four years unless they really liked you. Lily smiled proudly at her friend. How she longed for Dot to be happy. She had known such unhappiness in her life, hopefully that was all going to change now.

The flowers Dot was carrying threatened to engulf her. She was not very tall, only five feet and one and a half inches tall in her stocking feet. Both her bridesmaids were taller than her, but even they seemed to be struggling with their huge bouquets of tulips. It was all the rage at the time to have enormous wedding bouquets; Dot guessed it was a reaction to the austere war years, as well as everyone trying to copy the magnificent bouquet Princess Elizabeth had carried on her wedding day.

Even those tall, gangly women on Ben's side of the church seemed impressed. She had never met his aunties before. They were all pretty intimidating looking, much taller and louder than their little sister Lou, Ben's mum. Still, she supposed there would be plenty of time to get to know them after the wedding.

"Dearly beloved..."

Dot smiled at the young man standing alongside her. How handsome he looked. Standing upright, as upright as he used to stand when he was in the Royal Air Force. Today, he was wearing a smart navy blue pinstripe suit with a white carnation in his lapel. Next to him stood his best mate, Ernest. Since meeting at the cycle club, they had become the best of friends—they had similar temperaments. Ernest completely understood that he was second choice as best man, for if Sid, Ben's childhood friend, hadn't been killed in the war, it would have been him standing at the altar instead.

For their honeymoon, Dot and Ben spent a few days down in Torquay at a little bed and breakfast place. It was run by the mother of a pilot who had served with Ben during the war.

"Mum will be happy to have you. Business has been a bit quiet since the war ended. Not much money around, I suppose? She'll give you a good rate. Mind you, she's a bit old fashioned, so she likes all her guests to be on time for their meals and stuff like that. But she's a good cook, so I'm sure you'll have a lovely time."

And of course, they did have a good time. They were young, newly married, madly in love, and happy to be alive after the dreadful war years in which so many others hadn't survived.

They saw all the sights of Torquay and strolled for hours along the seafront in the pouring rain. Luckily, Dot had included a smart raincoat with a hood in her packing, so she was able to keep warm and dry, despite the showers. The couple was just happy to be together, away from everything they knew and in such a beautiful part of the world.

Their landlady did indeed provide them with delicious meals, so they had to walk long distances each day just to work off their enormous breakfast and make room for the scrumptious dinners they knew to expect. It seemed that they had not been quite so affected by the strictures of food rationing in Torquay as they had been in London.

One evening, Ben decided it would be fun to take Dot to the theatre. He knew how much she loved going to shows. She used to go to them all the time in London—sometimes with him, if there was something he fancied seeing, but more often she went with her friend Lily or her Aunty Rose. He didn't mind either way; he just loved seeing his girl happy.

Anyway, it turned out there was a good show at the Pavilion Theatre, so without telling Dot, he asked the landlady to book them some tickets. He even gave her an extra four pence to buy a programme; he knew Dot would love that. She had quite a collection of programmes at home in an old shoe box, from all the shows she had been to over the years.

The show ended up running late due to all the encores. The actors came back on stage several times to bow again to their appreciative audiences. The theatre was packed. Although it was late March and rather miserable and chilly at night, it seemed that half the population of Torquay wanted to be entertained.

It was late when they got back to the little guesthouse, and the place was in total darkness.

"Let's just throw a stone up at the window. That'll wake the old girl up. She probably thought we were back already, otherwise she wouldn't have locked up. Shame we didn't ask her for a key."

Dot refused to let him throw stones. She was cross with him for insisting they hang around until the very end of the show. She had known it would take them a while to walk back and had noticed the signs on the front door of the B&B saying, "*This door will be securely locked at 9.30pm nightly. Please tell the management if you intend to stay out late, and they will provide you with a key.*"

They had their first row standing on the doorstep in the pouring rain. Dot was hoping that someone would hear and let them in, but the house remained in darkness despite their gentle knocking. Eventually, they realised they could be standing there all night, so they decided to walk back into town to find another place to stay. All their possessions, apart from what they were wearing, were in the little room at the B&B. Having trudged the streets and finding no cheaper places still open, they were forced to book into the Grand Hotel–the seaside town's most expensive hotel. Dot was very embarrassed for looking rather dishevelled in her wet raincoat, her small handbag being her only piece of luggage. The hotel porter was very kind, escorting them to their rather smart bedroom, acting as if all his clientele were young honeymooners with barely a penny to their name. He kindly advised them–as he flung open the door to their splendid bedroom overlooking the sea–that a *"delicious breakfast is included in your room price, and will be served from 7am to 10am. Enjoy your night in our lovely hotel."* He winked at Ben as he left, obviously imagining that this handsome young couple would have a very romantic night in their luxurious room.

Poor Ben never got to enjoy the delicious inclusive breakfast, as Dot insisted they leave the hotel at 7am the next morning–before they had even had a cup of tea in the smart dining room.

"Oh, Ben, she'll be so worried. She'll think something dreadful has happened to us if we don't appear at breakfast."

Their landlady just laughed. *"Oh, my dear, I'm so sorry. I slept so soundly I just didn't hear you knock. I doubt I would even have heard if you'd thrown stones at the window. I just assumed you were home. Of course, with you being newlyweds, I wouldn't dream of knocking on your door to check."*

Ben had been keen to walk back into town, to claim the all-inclusive breakfast they'd been promised, but Dot was too embarrassed. It had been bad enough turning up at the smart hotel late at night, looking like a drowned rat with no luggage. There was no way she was going back there, even for a posh breakfast!

Of course, that unplanned expense put quite a dent in Ben's wallet, so the rest of their honeymoon week was not as extravagant as he had planned. It made no difference, though. Dot and Ben were in love, and so happy to be starting their new life together.

The first few years were great. Ben was thrilled to be free, to be his own man, to come and go as he pleased. After the structure the war had imposed on them all, he was happy to have a very flexible type of structure in his life. He had a wife he adored, a job he loved, and he was taking evening classes to get more qualifications that could hopefully get him an even better job in the future. He was still living at home with parents who adored him. He and Dot were out at work all day, so it was great that his mum was happy to clean the house, do the laundry, and cook all the meals. He thought it was absolutely perfect, the ideal life.

"Ben, I'm a bit fed up. I wish we had our own place."

"Oh don't be silly, Squibs. If we did, you'd have to do all your own cooking and cleaning. Just think how tired you'd be having to do all that after a hard day's work."

"But sometimes I don't think your mum likes me much. I think she preferred it when she had you all to herself."

Ben raised his eyebrows. Not this again! He'd been hearing this for weeks now. What did she expect him to do about it? There weren't any houses to rent; so many of them had been destroyed in the Blitz. Anyway, he was quite happy living with his mum and dad. He didn't understand why she wasn't.

"At least you go out to work every day, Squibs. You were lucky they let you stay on after the wedding."

It was true. Most firms insisted that married women stayed at home; that was, apparently, where they belonged. Although it was 1950 and many women had been considered "good enough" to contribute to the war effort, post war, once again, they were only thought to be good enough for house-work and childbearing.

Sadly, Dot would probably never be a mother. She had been told that her childhood illnesses and operations meant she would never be able to bear children. This news had come as a great blow to her; she had always loved little ones and ex-pected to have a family of her own one day. She had so looked forward to being a mother, to becoming the kind of loving mother she had always dreamt of having herself.

On the day Ben proposed, Dot had told him the news, expecting him to take back his offer of marriage. To her sur-prise, he had said instead:

"Oh Dot, it's you I want. I don't care if we don't have a brood of kids. We can be happy, just the two of us. I know we can. And if you start to get too broody, we can always think about adop-tion. There's plenty of babies who need a good home."

And so they spent the first few years living with Ben's parents, sharing his old bedroom. Luckily, Dot had very few possessions of her own, so although the room was a little crowded, the two were in love and just happy to be together. The walls were a bit thin, so it was hard to get much privacy, but they looked forward to Saturday evenings when his parents went to the cinema. That gave them a few precious hours to have the house to themselves.

They often met up after work and went to the pictures or the theatre. Sometimes, if they were feeling flush after payday, they would even treat themselves to dinner at Lyons Corner House.

After a couple of years, they decided it was time to have a family. They registered with an adoption agency and went to various children's homes to see the babies who needed new parents. They had passed all the tests and fulfilled all the requirements when Dot began to feel unwell. At first, she thought it was just a bit of food poisoning–maybe the fish they'd eaten the night before was off? But after a few weeks, she realised there was something more. Without mentioning anything to Ben, she made an appointment with her doctor.

"Promise me you won't tell your mum yet. Not until I start showing. Not 'til we're sure everything's okay with the baby."

He couldn't keep it to himself. He was so thrilled. Ben had never expected to be a dad–not to a baby of his very own. Of course he would have been happy to adopt one of those poor little mites that needed homes. He felt a bit guilty giving up on that path, but perhaps one day, when they were more established, they could think about adopting a couple of kids to add to their family.

Meanwhile, Dot was exhausted. They were having an Indian summer. It was so hot for late September, and the train journey home had been awful. She hadn't even managed to get a seat and had had to stand the whole way. Now her feet hurt and her ankles were all puffy. She couldn't wait to get home and take off her shoes.

The front door flung open just as she was about to put her key in the lock.

"So, I hear you're pregnant."

As they lay in bed that night, she sobbed in Ben's arms.

"Your mum hates me. I know she does. She didn't even say congratulations about the baby. She just said 'Oh, I hear you're pregnant.' She made me feel like some little kid who'd got into trouble."

In the bedroom opposite, another conversation was taking place.

"Maybe you should just apologise to the girl. You did sound a bit harsh. Not the response she was expecting, not like an excited Granny. No wonder she was upset."

"Well, I was just a bit surprised. I didn't even know they were trying for a baby. I thought Ben said that 'cos of a few problems she'd had when she was a youngster, she probably wouldn't be able to have kids of her own. He told me the other day that they'd been thinking about adoption instead. So it was a bit of a shock, that's all."

"I know, love. But I really do think you should apologise to the girl for being so rude. Don't forget, she hasn't got a mum or a sister, and I don't think she gets on too well with that hard faced sister-in-law of hers."

Sadly, Lou never apologised to Dot. Like all things left unsaid in life, the resentment began to fester.

By the time baby Ann was born, four months later, the two women were barely talking. They exchanged pleasantries, even went shopping together a few times to buy things for the baby, but when Ben and Eustace were not around, they hardly said a word to each other.

Dot had to stay at home all day with the baby. She had been forced to give up her job after giving birth. Although women like her had contributed hugely to the war effort, once they were married, they were considered "*just housewives who should know their place and be happily tied to the kitchen sink.*" Although she loved her baby dearly, she rather resented having to give up her freedom. She had loved travelling up to the city every day, loved the camaraderie of the little sewing room, and loved earning her own money, feeling like an independent woman.

Despite the tension and drama, the entire family adored baby Ann. She was a pretty blonde-haired little thing, the apple of everyone's eye.

Ben was a great father. He took his girl on long walks—at first in her pram, then holding her hand tightly after she learnt to toddle along on her own little feet.

Ann was a joy to them all, whether she was singing nursery rhymes at the top of her lungs, washing and pegging out her dollies clothes on the line, or helping her grandad, Eustace, pick flowers from his garden to go on the mantelpiece.

Ben was content. He had all he longed for. A pretty, clever wife, a beautiful little daughter. A good job and a comfortable home. In some ways, his life hadn't really changed that much since getting married; he just had two more people to love. Of course, he wished that his mum and his wife got on better, but surely, in time, Dot would realise that living with his mum and dad wasn't so bad after all. He knew she missed going up to town every day, missed having a job and money of her own, but he was sure that as their little Ann got bigger, she would have her hands so full that she would settle down and be happy. Maybe in time they would even have another baby!

The Festival of Britain had been held in 1951, a much-needed boost to the country and its people after the austerity of the war and the years of rationing that followed. Life had become rather drab, and so this festival, "*designed to promote a feeling of recovery and be a beacon for change*," was well received. It went on for several months and Dot and Ben took little Ann up to Lambeth to see all the new buildings that had been created on the South Bank. On a 27-acre site where old buildings had been completely bombed out, there now arose new constructions, modern designs that would feature in the post-war rebuilding of London and the establishment of new towns elsewhere. The splendid new Royal Festival Hall and many other modernist buildings were built for the festival.

Dot and Ben also took baby Ann to the new Pleasure Gardens in Battersea Park a few times, and always popped in to see the Cloke family while they were in town. Lily and Edgar were thrilled that their matchmaking had been so satisfactory. They were still both single themselves, but lived with the hope of falling in love one day, just like their friends Dot and Ben had done. Lily had been thrilled when Dot asked her to be godmother to little Ann, always remembering to send her a small gift for her birthdays and at Christmas.

Princess Elizabeth became the Queen of England after the death of her beloved father, King George VI. The whole country celebrated her coronation in 1953. It was yet another happy event the country needed after the grey sadness of the war years. There were tea parties in every village and town throughout the country with fancy dress competitions for adults and children. Everyone was thrilled when two-year-old Ann won second prize, wearing an outfit Dot had made from crêpe paper. It had been a last-minute effort, as she had been hoping she, Ben, and Ann could go to the street party at her old home in Morden, but her sister-in-law put the kibosh on that. Jean told Valentine not to bother inviting them, as *"they have probably already made other plans."* Valentine George, that quiet, gentle man, was not strong enough to stand up to his rather fierce daughter-in-law. She seemed to have completely taken over his home, to the point of making him feel so uncomfortable that he agreed to move out of his big front bedroom to the smaller room at the back of the house. His three-year-old granddaughter was already occupying Dot's old room, the second-biggest bedroom. At least his new room overlooked the garden, so he could lie in bed and look out at the little space he had so lovingly planted when they first moved to the house back in the 1930s.

He never could have imagined then that it would come to this some twenty years later–being made to feel like a rather unwelcome stranger in his own home. A home that he was still paying the rent on!

Sometimes Valentine worried dreadfully about Dot. He often thought that he should have stood up for her more, not let that daughter-in-law of his make his girl feel so unwelcome in her own childhood home.

He knew that she wasn't really happy living with her in-laws at Rose Hill. They were nice enough people, but his girl had always been quite shy and sensitive. Although she never complained, he could tell she wasn't happy. She loved her baby, of course, it had been such a surprise to them all when she announced she was pregnant. After her first operation—at home, on the kitchen table when she was just a toddler—the doctor had taken her father aside and said that her chances of carrying a baby in the future were very slim. In those days, doctors were gods, so ordinary folk like him never questioned them. They never asked for reasons, but rather were just grateful that the men in white coats had managed to save the lives of their loved ones. Of course they hadn't managed to save Lily, his first wife, Dot's mother, who had died just before her 31st birthday. That had been before this new National Health Service, a marvellous thing that meant poor people were no longer frightened to call the doctor, worried about spending sixpence they couldn't afford.

He was glad Dot had had her baby in that big new hospital at Rose Hill. At least he knew she would be safe there. St. Helier Hospital had a great reputation, although if you listened to Dot, you'd have thought it was the Workhouse.

"I am never ever going to have another baby in that hospital. If I am lucky enough to expect again, it will be born at home, in my own bed. Do you know, from the minute they examined me and said I was definitely in labour, they put me in a room all on my own and told me to ring a bell when the pain got worse? So I did, and the horrible midwife came and told me not to make a fuss, that the baby was hours away yet. So I stayed in that room,

on my own, all night, trying not to cry out and only rang the bell about 8 o'clock in the morning, once I thought I was going to pass out with the pain. Then they told me off for not calling sooner. Ann was born just an hour later."

Valentine was so sad listening to this. If only he had been allowed to be with her. But of course, it wasn't acceptable for fathers to be there when a woman gave birth. They were just supposed to pace the hospital corridors anxiously, then pop in and visit mother and baby when they were all cleaned up and presentable, before going off to celebrate the baby's birth with their mates. His poor Dot hadn't even had a mother or sister around to comfort her. It made his heart break, she deserved so much more.

When little Ann was three and a half years old, everything changed. By now, Dot and Ben had been living with his parents for almost six years, and the strain was beginning to tell on their relationship. Dot tried hard to remain positive, to enjoy her little family and make the best of their situation, but it was hard. She often day-dreamed about her years in the army, her years of being free and single without a care in the world–if you discounted the fact that the war in Europe was causing havoc and misery all around! She often looked at the old black and white photos of her and all the other girls on their searchlight sites. These were photos that showed her looking ridiculously young in her army uniform, with a tanned face covered in a mass of freckles from being outside in the sunshine. She really felt as though those years had been the happiest of her life; she had been free to dream and imagine a wonderful, glorious life. A life of travel, adventure, and fun—not a life where she was stuck in one tiny bedroom with her lovely husband, her adorable daughter, and her not so lovely in-laws.

She realised she was being unfair to dislike them. After all, they were providing her and her family with a home and they did try to be nice to her. She just couldn't get over how Lou, her mother-in-law, had been so rude when she was pregnant. Although the older woman tried hard to be kind and obviously really loved her little granddaughter, Dot just couldn't forgive her for being so unfeeling. She did realise that perhaps she was overreacting a little, but because she had never had the luxury of a mother or sisters as she grew into a woman, she was unable to cope with the normal drama and strife a family life often holds.

By the time 1954 came round, Dot and Ben were expecting their second baby and were going to be moving into their very own house, a brand new council house in the country, miles away from the smog and grime of the city.

Their new house in Surrey was a bog-standard council house set in a street of identical brick built houses. There were no frills, but all the basics needed for a family. Two small bedrooms, a tiny bathroom with a sink, toilet, and bath, and a narrow hallway downstairs that opened into a small kitchen. There was also a sitting room which overlooked a little garden. The garden was surrounded by low wire fencing, so although it determined the exact size of each plot, it gave no privacy from your neighbours. Dot didn't care about any of this, she was just happy to have her own home at last—a place where she and Ben could establish their family properly. A place where they could be happy, away from her mother-in-law.

She knew she was being a bit unreasonable. After all, her in-laws, Lou and Eustace, had provided them with a home for nearly six years, willingly sharing their small house with their son, his wife, and their little granddaughter. But Dot had never been truly happy there. She had always felt like an outsider, never really part of the family circle. She realised that it wasn't all her mother-in-law's fault, but she hated it when Ben defended his mum, especially when she, his wife, was unhappy and crying.

"Oh love. She didn't mean it, I'm sure. Mum doesn't really have a bad bone in her body, she's just a bit sharp sometimes. I think it's because she grew up with all those sisters. I remember they were always bickering and arguing when I was young, when we all lived in Peabody Buildings. You're just not used to the rough and tumble of family life. She doesn't mean to hurt you, I'm sure she doesn't."

But his words did not console Dot. She just seethed quietly, resenting each word her mother-in-law spoke, seeing fault in her every action. Living in the same small space made it easy for her dissatisfaction to escalate. Everything Lou did annoyed her.

Dot realised she was being unfair; both of Ben's parents adored their son and just wanted the best for him. But she also knew that, although they liked her, they thought he could have done better than marry a rather sensitive, motherless girl.

Of course, they all adored little Ann. Eustace had hung a little washing line in his precious garden especially low so she could reach it herself, to peg out her dollie's clothes once she had carefully washed them in the bucket of soapy water Lou had given her. Eustace had even made a little wooden swing to hang in the apple tree. He went out there most summer evenings when he got home from work to push his little granddaughter endlessly, higher and higher as she squealed with delight, until Dot shouted that it was time for them to come in and wash their hands for tea.

"Mum, Dad. We have some news. We're expecting another baby at Christmas."

Ben couldn't hide his pride. Having married Dot knowing she was unlikely to have children of her own, he was thrilled to be becoming a father for a second time. It had really surprised him how much love he felt for little Ann, and he knew he was going to love their second baby just as much. Of course, he was a bit worried about how they were going to manage financially now that Dot had had to give up her tailoring job, but she had assured him it would all be fine. His little Squibs. How he loved her. That wife of his was the best thing that ever happened to him. He was just sad that she and his mum didn't get along better–the two most important women in his life, constantly at each other's throats.

"Congratulations, Son. And you too, Dot."

Lou had learnt her lesson. First time around, when they had announced they were expecting little Ann, she knew she hadn't behaved well. Eustace often nagged her about it. This time she was determined to do better.

"Of course, it will be a bit of a squeeze. But we'll manage somehow."

Dot's voice was unusually loud when she replied.

"Oh, you don't have to worry about that. We're getting out of your hair. We've been given a council house. Near Epsom Downs. We can move in next month, so we'll be all settled by the time the baby arrives."

"Oh. Well I guess if you're moving out to the country, at least there won't be a Woolworths."

Lou didn't mean to speak so harshly, but she was shocked. Shocked that Ben and his little family would be leaving her. She had become so used to having them around. Apart from the war years when he had been in South Africa, her boy had never been away from home, away from his mother's loving care. Now she was going to lose her little granddaughter, and the new baby too.

"Oh come on, Mum. We don't have to go over that again." Ben spoke sadly. He hated it when his mum criticised Dot. He just wished that the two most important women in his life could get along.

Dot blushed. Her mother-in-law was right for once, which made it all the more terrible.

When baby Ann was small, just to get out of the house, Dot had pushed her pram all the way to Sutton. It had been a long walk in the summer heat, taking more than 30 minutes to cover the mile-and-a-half-long journey. But it cleared her head and helped to get rid of the frustration and anger for a while. Going home on the bus a couple of hours later, she felt much brighter–almost as though a weight had been lifted from her mind.

"Where's the pram? Where's the baby?"

Dot had been horrified. She remembered she had left baby Ann sitting happily in her pram, smiling at all the passers-by while she had popped into Woolworths to buy some more wool to knit a little cardigan for her 2nd birthday. She wasn't alone, there were several prams lined up outside the shop. It wasn't big enough to fit them all inside, and everyone knew their babies would be safe sitting out there in the sunshine.

Unfortunately, on this occasion, Dot had been in a daydream and had completely forgotten to collect her baby after finishing her shopping. She had enjoyed the short bus journey home, staring happily out of the window, watching the world pass by. She did have a funny feeling that she had forgotten to buy something, but just couldn't remember what it was!

"I can't believe you've been so stupid. Leaving my granddaughter outside Woolworths. Whatever were you thinking of? Supposing someone's stolen her? She's such a pretty little thing. I'll never forgive you if something happened to her."

Dot had been utterly distraught and had rushed straight back to town on the next bus. Of course, little Ann was safe and sound, thoroughly enjoying her little adventure and being fussed over by everyone who passed by.

And now, Dot's wretched mother-in-law was bringing it up again.

1955. Surrey

They all loved the new house. Well, more or less.

Ben loved the fact that Dot was happier not being under the constant surveillance of his mum every day. She sang as she did the housework, keeping the little place spotlessly clean. He often joked that the floors were so clean after she'd swept and mopped them every day, that they didn't need to bother with the table. They could just eat their dinner off the floor! Each time he said this, little Ann agreed, just as long as she was still allowed to have a plate. She didn't want any creepy crawlies from the floor getting into her dinner— she had seen plenty of those when she was playing out in the back garden!

Little Ann rather hero-worshipped her dad. Whenever they went for a walk down the country lane behind their new house, she insisted on holding tightly onto Ben's hand, while Dot pushed the pram behind them. Dot smiled to herself as she watched them strolling along, both rather pigeon-toed, chattering nineteen to the dozen as they walked. Bits of their conversation filtered through the chilly autumn air.

"Dad, aren't we lucky to live in the country?"

"Do you think we'll see many animals today, or will the farmer have put them all in the barn to keep warm?"

"Can I stroke the horses?"

"Do you think Baby's warm enough? Did Mum put enough blankets on her?"

Ann had become a big sister just a few weeks before, when Dot gave birth to baby Carol, much earlier than expected. It had been a worrying time—the baby was so premature—but she was a little fighter. In no time at all, mother and baby were doing well enough to be sent home from the hospital. For little Ann, it was love at first sight. She became like a little mother, utterly protective of her baby sister.

Dot was content. At last, she had her own home, her lovely husband all to herself, and two adorable daughters. It all seemed like a bit of a miracle, really.

The only thing that was disappointing was the house. It was nice enough inside—everything was clean and modern—but she just wished they had been given one of the houses on the *other* side of the street. They were pretty much the same as hers inside, but they all had big picture windows facing the street. In these houses, you could sit in your front room and watch the world go by. Of course, it meant the families inside were in a bit of a fishbowl—everyone could peek in to see what kind of furniture and stuff they had. However, most of them got 'round that little inconvenience by hanging pretty net curtains on the window, that way they could still spy on everyone going past without people peering in at them!

"Oh love, why can't you just be happy with what we've got? It's a nice little house, much more modern than Mum and Dad's. You don't have to go through the kitchen to get to the bathroom, and the kitchen has got plenty of cupboards. There's even a shed in the garden for our coal, so it doesn't have to go in the hallway cupboard like it does at Mum's. She was so envious when she came here; I think she realises now that we didn't have any choice but to move out of the city. We could never have afforded a place like this in London."

Dot knew Ben was frustrated by her constant moaning. Whenever he was cross with her, he didn't use her nickname, "Squibs," he just called her "love" or "Dot."

"At least you are home all day and can enjoy this nice house. I have to get up at the crack of dawn every day, walk to the bus stop, and hang around for ages in the cold waiting for the bus to come. Then, I have to change buses again to get to the factory. Sometimes I have to run to make sure I get there on time."

Ben now worked at a new factory in Mitcham. It was affiliated with his old company, but had been set up especially to manufacture the new colour television sets that were becoming popular. Of course, it would be many years before every home in the country had such a luxury item in their home–many people in England still didn't even own a black and white set–but the owners of the company were certain that by the 1970s, everyone would want one.

It was not an easy journey for Ben to get to work every day. He would have much preferred to travel on his pushbike, but that really wasn't an option. The factory was just a bit too far for that to be practical. If only they were still at his mum and dad's in Rose Hill, it would be an easy 12-minute cycle ride. Still, he just had to keep his chin up and make the most of it. At least he could pop in and see his parents on a Saturday afternoon after he finished work. Sadly, Dot didn't seem keen to visit them. She made lots of excuses about it being "too cold to take the baby out," or how "Ann got fidgety waiting around at the bus stop after trudging there for twenty minutes on her little feet." She wouldn't even go to spend Christmas with them, saying she wanted to go to her family in Morden instead.

Ben refrained from pointing out that the bus journey to Morden was actually ten minutes longer than the one to Rose Hill, but inside, he was seething. He understood that she preferred spending time with her own family, but he hated that she seemed to be keeping his mum and dad at arm's length. After all, they had been the ones good enough to give them a home all those years. Apart from the occasional comment, he kept those thoughts to himself. He knew it was something of a tricky subject, and he certainly didn't want to make things worse.

"Father Christmas, where's my baby's present?"

The little girl looked accusingly at the old white-haired man in the red suit who was sitting in his grotto. He stifled a grin and whispered to the elf standing by his side. The elf shook her head. Dot was mortified. She had only paid for one ticket–baby Carol was only a couple of months old! She'd never know that there hadn't been enough money for her to see Father Christmas as well.

The old man, who, by this time was rather weary of dealing with numerous small children and their outlandish requests, was amused. How lovely that this little girl cared enough about her baby sister to tackle the great man. He nodded to the elf and she went to the sack labeled, *"Under 2 years."* He handed a brightly-wrapped gift to the little girl in front of him. She smiled and thanked him.

Outside the department store, Dot felt her face burning. Surely, someone was going to come and demand she pay another shilling for the extra present.

"See Mum, Father Christmas would have forgotten about Carol if I hadn't reminded him. Look at this nice rattle he gave her."

Ben laughed when Dot told him the story that evening. He loved it that Ann was so loving, loyal, and feisty.

In the end, they spent the whole of Christmas week with Dot's family in Morden, just popping over to Rose Hill on Boxing Day afternoon to visit Lou and Eustace.

"Ooh, it's so lovely to see you all. Come in, come in, it's freezing out there! Oh Ann, love, you look so pretty in that little hat and coat. Did your mum make it for you? She's so clever, isn't she? You certainly haven't lost your sewing touch, have you Dot? How's Baby Carol doing? Oh my, she's grown so much since I saw her last. Can you believe she wasn't meant to be born 'til this week? She was supposed to be a Christmas baby."

Finally, Lou paused for breath. She was so excited to see them all.

"Can I hold her?"

"Now Nanny, you have to be really careful. She's very small, so you must treat her gently."

Little Ann had gone into full big sister mode. She hovered behind Lou, making sure the baby's head was at exactly the right angle and that the lacy shawl was wrapped firmly around her little body.

"Nice shawl. Did you knit it, Dot?"

"No, it was a Christmas present from my brother and his wife. Jean is a really good knitter; we all got stuff she'd made as our Christmas presents."

"I got this cardigan, but Mum had to wash it before I could wear it, 'cos it smelt horrible."

They all laughed as Ann wrinkled up her little nose to show her distaste. They knew that Jean was a bit of a chain smoker, lighting one cigarette after another. The smell of nicotine got into all her clothes, even into the knitting she was constantly doing.

The afternoon passed pleasantly, and Ben was delighted to see that Dot was making a real effort to be nice. She let his mum hold the baby for ages, even his dad had a little cuddle, and of course, they both made a real fuss over little Ann. They missed their granddaughter terribly; until now, she had lived with them her whole life. They were used to spending time with her every day.

The visit was over far too soon for Ben, Lou, and Eustace, but Dot honestly couldn't wait to get away. She found the atmosphere rather claustrophobic, and however hard she tried to be nice, she got irritated by nearly everything her mother-in-law said. Little Ann cried when she had to say goodbye to her grandparents. She loved them and couldn't understand why she couldn't see them more often. Baby Carol behaved beautifully of course, she was happy to be the centre of attention for once. She was such a quiet, placid little thing, so easy to love.

That winter was long and cold. Every time Dot put the washing on the line in the garden, it would end up frozen. Ben's shirts would hang there looking like scarecrows. There was no heating in the little house, just a backburner next to the open coal fire to heat the water. They would all take turns standing in front of it in an attempt to get warm.

The days dragged on. It was often too cold and snowy for little Ann to play outside for long, so she would come indoors crying, her little fingers chilled through her woollen mittens. Dot would stop whatever she was doing to make a cup of tea for herself and some hot milk for the little girl, and they would curl up together on the settee. Baby Carol, who was a model baby, would usually be fast asleep in her pram in the corner of the room, so Dot would let her eldest daughter rest her little head on her mum's warm body and tell her a story. Dot loved making up stories. It seemed to satisfy a deep-seated need in her to be creative. Soon the little girl would be fast asleep, and Dot would pick up one of her own treasured books to read. Some of her books had been purchased when she first started work, others she had acquired during the war years.

Reading had always been a passion of hers, and thank goodness it was free! There was certainly no spare money to buy books these days; everything Ben earnt got spent on the rent, insurances, electricity, gas, and his bus fares to work. Sometimes there was hardly any money left to buy food, so Dot had learnt to be really inventive. It was a good job that she had grown up poor, at least she knew how to make money stretch. But sometimes, she resented it. She resented having to watch every single penny, waiting for the gas and electricity man to come and empty the meter so she could get a little pile of shillings back if she'd put in too much. Those were real red letter days. Afterwards, she would put the baby in the pram, get Ann washed and dressed, and walk over to the shops at Burgh Heath to buy them all a few treats. Sometimes she would daydream about a day when she wouldn't have to penny pinch all the time. When she could go to the shops and buy a few lamb chops or some nice fresh fruit, even a new book for herself on occasion. Those daydreams kept her going.

As any new mother knows, life is very hard. It is hard to drag yourself out of bed in the morning after a night punctuated by a crying baby needing a feed. Hard to find time to get washed and dressed, to comb your hair, or eat a decent meal. Add to that a small, demanding toddler, a lack of money, frustration, loneliness, no family support, and a husband who is out working from dawn 'til dusk to feed his family. Without any other dramas, that lot in itself is enough to breed depression and despair.

While Dot was struggling at home, alone and rather miserable at times, Ben was fighting his own demons.

He loved his wife and daughters dearly, but he was tired. Tired of having to get up at the crack of dawn every day to travel to work. The work itself was easy; he was good at his job and appreciated by his workmates. He liked the camaraderie of the factory. In that respect he was just like his mum, Lou had always loved working in factories. She was more gregarious than him, but they shared the same love of life and interest in people.

He could have coped with the long journey to work if he didn't have to deal with all the issues at home. Dot tried not to moan, he knew she did, but as soon as he walked in the door, he could tell by her face that she was struggling.

"Hello, Squibs."

"I'm so glad you're back, Ben. Ann has been asking and asking 'when Daddy will be home.' She wanted to stay up to see you, but I told her she wasn't even four yet, so she had to be in bed by 6.30. She asked if, when she was five, she could stay up every night 'til you got home!"

Although Ben could see how irritated Dot was, it made him rather proud to think that his little girl wanted to stay up late just to see him.

"Can you take the baby, please? She hasn't stopped crying all day. I think she must be teething, it's not like her to be so miserable."

Ben lifted his youngest daughter out of the pram. Her little face was all red and screwed up. He kissed her gently on the nose and held her against his shoulder.

"Oh for goodness sake, Ben, take your coat off first. That rough wool will scratch her skin. And make sure your hands are warm."

"I'm afraid there's only egg and chips, and a bit of bread for your tea. There wasn't enough money left to buy any meat. Oh, and I need to pay the milkman tomorrow. He left a note saying he couldn't deliver any more until we settled the bill."

"*Oh no, there's Ann coming down the stairs, she must have heard your voice. Now we're never going to get her back to sleep unless we put her in our bed. You know how she gets frightened because she thinks there are crocodiles on the landing.*"

BEN'S BREAKDOWN

Ben tried so hard to hold it altogether, but in the end, it just became too much.

He had gone from being a happy young father of one with a pretty, loving wife and a job he enjoyed, still living in his parent's house and being protected from the harsh reality of the world. Just a few short months later, he now had the responsibility to maintain a house of his own, deep in the countryside, miles from his work, his parents, and everything he had always known. He had had an easy, comfortable life– until now.

Now, he had a rather unhappy wife, two little daughters, a long journey to work, and not enough money. He tried so hard to make it work, but eventually, he had a nervous breakdown.

He was hospitalised in the old buildings that had been turned into a mental hospital at Belmont in Surrey. The structures were built in the 1850s, originally to provide *"industrial training for poor children."* The bleak place then became a workhouse, where conditions were so harsh that in 1910, the inmates rioted. During World War I, it had been used as a hospital for German prisoners of war and as an internment camp for *"civilian enemy aliens awaiting repatriation."* In 1922, it reverted to being a workhouse, but conditions remained very poor. Apparently, it was filthy and rat-infested. During World War II, it became the Sutton Emergency Hospital, used to treat trauma patients and war casualties. In 1946, it was renamed the Belmont Hospital, specialising in psychiatric medicine. At all points in history, it was a place of dread. A place no one ever hoped to go, either as a visitor or as a patient. In 1950s Britain, mental illness still carried such a stigma.

"My dad's been in there for ages. I wish he would come home soon."

Ann's little voice trilled across the top deck of the bus as she pointed to the old hospital on the hill. Dot sunk down into the seat. She was mortified and looked around furtively, hoping no one had heard the little girl speak.

Ten minutes later, she stood up to get off the bus. Her face was still flushed; she was holding tightly onto Ann's hand and clutching Baby Carol in her arms. She just couldn't wait to get off, away from all the people who now knew her shameful story.

She collected the baby's folding pram from the bus conductor and climbed down onto the pavement. She was so hot and bothered that she didn't notice how cold it was outside. An old lady tapped her gently on the shoulder.

"Sorry to interrupt you, my dear, but I heard what your little girl said on the bus. I know what it's like, but you mustn't be ashamed. It's not your fault. So many of our boys came back

damaged from the war. Even if they didn't actually fight on the front lines, they've seen and heard terrible things–things that will haunt them forever. It's us who suffer most though, I reckon. We're the ones left behind to try and pick up the pieces, who try to keep the kids happy and well fed. My two boys both ended up in those places for months on end. It was bloody hard. No one would let their wives or kids visit them; they wouldn't even let me–the boys' own mother–in to check on them. The doctors said they would rehabilitate better without worrying about us. I feel for you, especially with those two bonny little ones. Still, I expect you've got plenty of family around to help, haven't you?"

Dot didn't have any family support and she was far too proud to ask anyone for help. She knew there were probably rumours flying around the street–rumours that Ben had left her or worse, but she kept her thoughts to herself. She didn't ever engage in conversation with any of her neighbours, apart from a quick nod and hello before rushing into the house.

It proved to be a very long six months while Ben was away. Six lonely months where Dot had no one but her children for company. Ben's firm paid him sick leave, so at least she could pay the rent and feed them, but there was certainly nothing left for luxuries. She even had to ask the milkman if she could pay him monthly instead of weekly, so she had a couple of extra days to balance the books.

She wasn't allowed to visit Ben, so every night she just sat alone, worrying. The girls were fast asleep upstairs, so at least they didn't see her crying hot, bitter tears. Tears for Ben and the awful predicament he was in, and tears for herself. This was nothing like the glorious, happy future they had planned when they were on their honeymoon just six years ago. How cruel life could be.

The doctors in charge of Ben's case had decided he would be a good candidate for their new electric shock therapy treatment, and he wrote to Dot explaining how it worked.

"Today I am having another session of treatment. It knocks you out a bit, so you have to stay in the Coma Ward where they can keep an eye on you afterwards—make sure you drink enough water and take glucose. They say I might be allowed to come home for a day visit in a few weeks time. Apparently the new doctor on the ward is very keen that married men with children don't get too isolated!"

Dot wrote to him almost every day while he was away.

"My Dearest Squibs,

It really was grand having you home for Easter, even though we never went anywhere. You see, my dear, even though you often make me unhappy, there could never be anyone but you. Being parted like we are, I realise just how much you mean to me. So here's looking to the future when your treatment is finished.

Wasn't the weather grand today? I did heaps of washing, then decided to attempt more digging in the garden. I soon got a nasty blister, guess all that washing clothes has made my hands too soft! Never mind, next time, maybe I shall wear gloves.

By the way, our coal arrived today, only five hundredweight though, as I couldn't afford more. Still, that's something.

I think baby Carol's teeth are beginning to worry her a little, though I must say, the cheeky monkey seems okay when

I nurse her. Ann has been really good today. Did you by any chance give her a pep talk? She certainly seems to have calmed down a little. I think she really misses having you around.

*The lady next door put her budgerigar's cage in the garden today and Ann informed me that said bird was a **parrot** and would not hear otherwise!*

Anyway, I must close now, as I have to write a few lines to Aunt Rose. I will say goodnight, my love. God Bless, and looking forward to seeing you again very soon. With lots of love from Ann, Carol and me, your loving Dot. xxxxx

P.S. Why have I written to you in pencil? Too much effort to walk into the kitchen for a pen!

Sometimes, Ben replied. Dot was always so happy when the little brown envelopes with his untidy writing plopped onto the doormat.

"Dearest Darling Dot,

Just finished my dinner after having the second treatment of the week. How is the baby getting on with her teething? Have you received your money from the National Health yet? The boys here just told me that after eight weeks, the patient's portion of the money (18 shillings) is reduced, so I guess you had better start preparing for the shortage. A couple of the chaps got a day pass on Saturday but didn't get back in time, so the police were called out!

Today the weather is dismal and almost everyone is just lying around on their beds or chairs. I have just read 'Doctor at Sea'; it is about sailors on a third-class cargo boat, written as though you are one of them, using their dos, don'ts, and slang. I have also been given a copy of 'Anna and the King of Siam.' They don't want it back, so if you'd like to read it, I can get it posted out to you.

Here's hoping to see you all soon. Please give my love to the girls.

Yours, Ben xxxxxxxxxxxxx

"My Dearest Squibs,

Hello my love, hope all is going well with you. Have just received your second H.S.F. benefit cheque for one pound, fifteen shillings, so will try to put that aside for the time being. The girls are fine, but we all miss you terribly. Please try and hurry home to us. Look after yourself and God Bless. All our love. As ever, Dot xxxxx

After six seemingly endless months, Ben finally came home. With him, he brought a rather nice wooden coffee table that he had made during his rehabilitation classes. Dot and the girls were thrilled to have him back, but his illness had left scars that changed their family dynamics forever.

The years passed and nothing much changed. Another baby—another little girl named Joanna—was added to the family. Dot hadn't really wanted another baby, at least not until they were a bit better off financially, but of course, contraception didn't always work. If only men were the ones having babies, she felt sure they would come up with some better, more reliable methods. Maybe by the time her girls grew up, the world would be a different place, maybe they would have

more chances to make their own decisions—not have motherhood forced on them whether they wanted it or not.

Every time she gave birth to another baby, Dot felt the loss
of her own mum. It hurt so much having no one with whom
to share the joys and pain of motherhood. Going into labour
in a clinical hospital bed, with no family support, was so hard.
The husbands were only allowed to pace the corridor and be
called in after the birth, when mum and baby were already
looking clean, shiny, and serene, so Ben had no real idea of
the agonies his wife had gone through.

*"Well I'll tell you this much, Ben. I've got no intention of
going back to that place to have this baby. This little one will be
born here, at home, not in that horrible hospital. I don't care
what you say, I'm not changing my mind."*

Ben was worried and confided in his father-in-law,
Valentine George, hoping the older man could persuade Dot
to change her mind.

A few months later, Valentine received this letter from
his mum Martha.

"My dear son, Valentine,

*I hope you are all well. I got a nice letter from your Dot
the other day telling me about her latest arrival. Three little
girls now! I wonder, do you think she was hoping for a boy this
time? Anyway, both she and the babe are well, which is the most
important thing. She said she had a home birth; apparently she
didn't want to go to the hospital this time. I don't understand
it. All the poor women in my day and for hundreds of years
before that would have given anything to give birth in a nice,*

clean hospital, instead of dying in the slums with only a single drunken midwife in tow. But I guess these young ones must think they know what they're doing. I'd just be worried if something went wrong and they couldn't get to the hospital in time.

Oh well, I guess it's just a sign of the changing times, it is 1956 after all! I've lived so long and seen so many changes that nothing much shocks me anymore. I reckon that people make the same mistakes now as they have done for centuries; no one seems to learn anything from history!"

Dot got used to being at home all day with her three little ones, but she was frustrated. Frustrated at not being able to provide them with everything they needed, and frustrated that all her days seemed to be the same. Boring, monotonous, lonely days, with not much to look forward to. She loved her children desperately–they and Ben were her whole world–but she just longed for more. Sometimes, when the housework was all done and the three girls were having a little afternoon nap, she would sit and daydream about the exciting life she had planned and dreamt of when she was a little girl. The big plans that she and Ben had talked about on their honeymoon. They were going to go on cycling adventures, not just in England, but maybe they'd even take their bikes on the cross channel ferry and cycle around the lanes of Northern France. They'd thought maybe one day, they'd manage to save up enough to travel *further* afield, to visit some of the places Dot had longed to see since she was a little girl.

She looked over at the wooden bookcase with the sliding glass doors. It was the one piece of furniture she had from her childhood home; it held all her treasures. Everything on those shelves held some special meaning to her. Her children knew it was forbidden to touch anything in there, it was all too precious. On the top shelf was an old ship in a bottle that John had made especially for her while he was serving on a minesweeper during the war. The little ship was named *THE LADY DOT*. Next to that was the old mandolin she had owned since the late 1930s. It was a beautiful thing made of solid silver. Her dad had bought it from an old Dutch refugee, and Dot had been so fascinated with it that, as soon as she started work and had money of her own, she offered to buy it from him. It was one of her most treasured possessions.

There were copies of her favourite books, including *Perfume from Provence, The Intelligent Woman's Guide to Socialism and Capitalism, The Water-Babies, Peter Pan and Wendy,* several leather-bound poetry books, and a few dog-eared old copies of Reader's Digest.

There was also a pile of books she had bought during the war, including *Testament of Youth* and *Dark Tide*, both by Vera Brittain. She had sheet music of *Polonaise* by Chopin, *The Story Of My Life* by Queen Marie of Roumania, *Destination Chungking* by Han Suyin, and *I Haven't Unpacked* by William Holt. Additionally, copies of *A Harp in Lowndes Square* by R. Ferguson and *Intelligence* by S.T. Felstead decorated the shelves. Looking at them was like looking at a different life, a life full of hope and promise.

On the bottom shelf lay all of Dot's notebooks and sketch pads. She didn't do much drawing lately–the girls kept her too busy–but occasionally, if she could persuade them to sit still, she would do little portraits of them. Nothing like her Uncle Albert could have done, of course, he had been a truly marvellous artist. But he had taught her well and she really wished she could show him her latest efforts. She had been so sad when he died, but at least he had met her little Ann. She would never forget seeing him in that hospital bed, his face and body so badly burned after the accident[1], tears running down his cheeks as he cuddled his little niece in his arms for the first–and last–time. He died the next day. She missed him still.

There were a few more books on the other shelves–some library books and a few of Ben's magazines, which he had sneaked in without her noticing. Every time she saw them, she got irritated. Somehow they looked so out of place in her nice bookcase, a pile of well-thumbed copies of *Radio Constructor*, a magazine from 1950 with articles such as: "Television Picture Faults, part 1" and "Rebuilding the R1155." Inside the black and orange covers were multiple adverts for receivers, transformers, electrostatic voltmeters, and valves. Ben spent copious amounts of time reading these magazines, which cost one shilling and threepence each time. Dot felt they were an extravagance the family could do without. Sometimes, when he wasn't around, she would sneak an occasional peek inside them, just to see what was so fascinating. In one article that caught her attention, she saw: "*Inexpensive Television* is the

---

[1]   As mentioned in *Valentine George*, book one of the Ancestors series, Uncle Albert had a fit of epilepsy and fell onto a fire, thus burning much of his body.

title of a booklet describing how to make a televisor for the London or Birmingham frequencies using ex- govt. radar material. Send only 1/9 to cover cost and postage for a copy, and also price list of material required." On the back page was a full-page advertisement for "CLYDESDALE SUPPLY CO., Bargains in Ex-Services Radio and Electronic Equipment." It made her rather sad to read about an *Ex-Army Supply Unit Rectifier for No. 43 transmitter"* and *"4-valve superhet chassis."*

Once, during the war, this kind of stuff had been her life. Now, every day was all about washing, cooking, and child-minding. Hard to find much mental stimulation there, although she did get a kind of thrill when, at six-thirty each morning, after Ben had left for work and while the girls were still upstairs sleeping, she had already swept and mopped the floors, dusted the few bits of furniture they had with nice lavender polish, laid the fire ready to be lit, and put some washing in the big copper boiler. Some days, she even managed to sit down with a nice cup of tea before she heard the girls stirring. She loved her cups of tea; sometimes she thought they were her biggest vice. Dot had never smoked or been much of a drinker, but she did love her tea–as long as it was nice and strong. "Strong enough to stand your spoon in it," her dad always used to say.

Some days she was content, happy even, with her life. Loving Ben and the girls was enough, it really was. At the same time, there was always a slight sadness, a shattered dream of how her life "should have" turned out–a life full of fun, friendship, and excitement. She knew that none of it was Ben's fault; he always did his very best to provide for her and the girls. But there was still something missing, an ache that just wouldn't go away, however tightly she hugged her children. She wanted so much more for them all.

Dot had tried to make friends on the new estate, but somehow she hadn't found it easy. It was almost as though she was back to being a quiet, unconfident little girl, a girl with no certainty that people would even like her enough to want to be her friend. The new neighbours were nice enough, but so far, she hadn't managed more than a brief chat over the garden fence. They all seemed older and more settled in their lives. It didn't seem as though they were struggling financially like her family was. She felt a bit like a fish out of water, and fleetingly wished they had never left Rose Hill. Sometimes, she wished they were still staying with Ben's mum and dad; at least then, she wouldn't be all alone trying to cope with everything. Not to mention, Ben probably wouldn't have had a nervous breakdown if they were still living there. That was a guilt she would carry forever–the thought that she had somehow let him down, pushed him into moving, into a situation he just couldn't cope with.

She had changed so much too. She was no longer the happy, carefree young girl she had been in the army. She was not the girl with big dreams anymore. Now, she could never envisage those dreams becoming a reality. If she couldn't even afford to buy a new pair of shoes for her daughter, how was she ever going to have enough money for her family to explore the world?

The years ticked by with no real change. The girls got bigger, it would soon be time for them, well, Ann at least, to start school. That meant more expenses and more worry. Dot was sick of worry. She began to resent Ben a little–resented his freedom and the fact that he could just walk out of the house every morning and go off to work, leaving her alone with the children. She resented him for all the interesting people he would meet each day; he was such a friendly chatterbox that it took him no time at all to make new acquaintances. He was always coming home talking about the people he met on the bus, in the factory, or at the shops. Dot, on the other hand, only saw the tally man, the insurance man, the travelling butcher, the baker, and the milkman, and even if she *were* confident enough to start up a conversation, none of them ever had much time to chat. She had tried joining the Young Wives Club at the local church, but didn't find anyone there whom she felt could truly become a friend. Overshadowing it all, of course, was the shame of having had her husband in the mental hospital. She was sure that some of those women whispered behind her back. It made her feel so uncomfortable that after a couple of months, she decided not to go back.

One day, out of sheer desperation, she put a little postcard in the newsagent's window:

"London-trained tailoress willing to do small sewing jobs."

Suddenly, it was like the floodgates were opened. Word quickly got around and soon, she had women turning up on her doorstep.

"Could you make me a dress for my sister's wedding? Maybe a matching jacket, too?"

"My Bert's lost a lot of weight, can you take all his trousers in?

"I bought this new coat up West, but it's too long. Can you shorten it?

"My daughter is getting married next year, can you make her dress? Oh, and there will probably be six bridesmaids ones to make, too."

Although it was hard work, especially with a home and three young children to care for, Dot began to thrive. It was so good to be doing a bit of sewing again. She often had to sit up all night to get a job finished, and Ben began to get anxious.

"Oh, Squibs. Are you really sure this is all worth it? It's making you worn out, I'm worried that you're taking on too much. Of course, I know it means you're bringing in a bit of money, which really helps, but I do think some of these people are taking advantage of your good nature. You could charge them a lot more, you know."

Dot got angry. How dare he tell her what to do!

"Listen, Ben, I don't tell you you're not being paid enough for what you do. If that company paid you just a bit more, more like what you're worth, we wouldn't be struggling so much and I wouldn't have to be taking up all these sewing jobs. Do you really think I like shortening old men's trousers or sewing in extra elastic to ladies' skirts so they can still wear them, even when they've put on a few pounds? Well, I can tell you it's not much fun. I'm worth more than that. I used to sew fine clothes for foreign royalty."

She sank back into the chair and stifled a sob.

"I hate this, being poor all the time."

Ben stood in front of her, trying not to cry. He wanted to take her in his arms, to tell her it was all going to be okay. But he couldn't. He knew that unless they won the football pools, or some long-lost relative died and left them a lot of money, nothing was going to change. They would be struggling year in, year out. He just couldn't see any way around it.

"I'm sorry, love. I think I'll just go out to the shed for a minute."

He didn't want her to see him cry. All the rehabilitation classes he had taken at the mental hospital said he must distance himself from difficult situations, otherwise he might risk a relapse.

They had two garden sheds, both brick-built to match the house. The first one held their coal, sacks of it ready to go on the open fire. It was delivered whenever they could afford it by lovely old Jack the Cockney coalman, with his horse and cart.

The other one was supposed to be the tool shed, somewhere to store the push along lawn mower, the garden tools, and Ben's bike. They only had one bike now; Dot had sold hers a couple of years ago, when he had been away in hospital and she had been rather desperate for money. He remembered being so upset when he came back and found it missing.

Ben sat in the dark shed and wept. It was never meant to be like this. He loved Dot and his girls so much and hated that he couldn't give them everything they needed and deserved. He felt like a failure–as a man, a husband, and a father.

Even despair becomes a kind of normality. Somehow, people accept that things are never going to get any better, so they learn to adapt and find pleasure in the small things.

Dot and Ben still loved each other deeply, and of course, they both loved their children unconditionally. They wanted to make sure that their girls felt loved, safe, and happy, and to their credit, they managed to put their misery aside to ensure that in their home.

They had no spare money, so they would often go for long family walks, over the Heath or to Epsom Downs where the girls could run around and play. On the rarest of occasions, if they had a few pennies extra, they would stop at a little café and buy the girls an ice cream. These were happy outings, although sometimes, Dot was too tired to really enjoy them—especially if she had been up late the previous night sewing. The girls were always tired on the long walk home, so Ben would give Ann a piggyback, while little Carol would get a lift in the baby's pram.

If it was a Sunday, they would give the girls their tea and a bath, then switch on the radio for *Sing Something Simple*. Dot and Ben would waltz around the room to the tunes being played whilst the girls watched. It was a very happy time for them all, creating special memories that would last forever.

To help with the family budget, Ben got an extra job working weekends at the little Shell garage in Burgh Heath. They were delighted to have him, a young, strong man who not only served the petrol, but could lend a hand mending the cars if necessary. Ben loved it; it was another chance to get out of the house, socialise, and earn extra money. Of course, it meant Dot was alone with the children even more, giving her less time to do her sewing. She was also annoyed because he had decided to take some evening classes, which meant he went straight from work to the technical college in the evenings.

"But I don't understand, Ben. Don't you think it's a bit selfish, doing something <u>else</u> for yourself when I'm stuck at home all day? Maybe I'd like to do some evening classes, too? I used to have lots of dreams, you know."

"Oh and by the way, I can't believe how much stuff you've got in that shed. Where on earth did all those old radios come from?"

He looked a bit sheepish.

"Oh, Ernest gave them to me. He dropped them off last weekend when you went to Morden to see your dad. Apparently they were being chucked out at his work, so he said he had a friend who was a whizz with radios who could probably fix them up."

"So are you going to?"

"Going to what?"

"Fix them up, silly?"

"Oh, yeah. I will. Just not quite yet. I've got those assignments to do for my evening class first. But I will get 'round to it. I promise they won't be in there long."

Five years later, they were still there. In fact, the little shed was now full to the brim, overflowing with more radios needing repair, a pile of old wooden-handled tools, and a couple of broken television sets.

That wasn't all. Every available space in the house was filled with Ben's stuff–even the cupboard in the bedroom the girls shared.

Little Ann had been indignant.

"But Dad, I don't understand. Why can't we keep our clothes and toys in that cupboard? It is our room, after all. You've got all your sheds and the cupboard in the <u>other</u> bedroom full of your

stuff. Why can't we have a bit of space? Anyway, me and Carol looked, and it's all just junk. Just junk! You should throw it out."

Ben was horrified, both at the fact that his precious daughter was telling him off *and* at her suggestion that his stuff was junk.

"It's not junk, love. Those are really good televisions, I just need to make a few alterations. Then, they'll be good as new. And all those magazines are collector's items. People will pay a fortune for those one day."

The magazines he was talking about were huge piles of Radio Constructor and similar titles, some dating back as far as 1948.

ANOTHER BABY

The three girls were all at school by now. In fact, Ann, now aged 11, had just started at the "big school"—a brand new edifice that had been built only a year ago.

Dot was a bit disappointed. She had always hoped her girl would be able to go to Rosebery Grammar School in Epsom. Of course, that would have meant an extra expense, paying for a posh uniform and all the bus fares and everything, but she would have done anything to give her girl a chance to do better—better than she herself had been able to do. She had been so proud when Ann passed her eleven-plus exam, and it seemed certain that she would be offered a place at Rosebery. Unfortunately, it turned out there were too many applicants that year. As Ann lived right opposite the new school, the education authority deemed she should go there instead. De Burgh was an experimental school, a forerunner of the later secondary moderns. Apparently they had a very good grammar stream and the headmaster was a Cambridge don.

On her first day there, Ann came home in tears.

"Oh Mum, I wish I could go back to Shawley Way."

Shawley Way Primary School at Epsom Downs was where her other siblings still went, and where Ann had attended since she was six years old. She started going there after the little church school at Burgh Heath had closed down. She had always been quite happy at both places, so Dot had assumed Ann would enjoy the new school too.

"Mum, it's horrible. I don't fit in."

Dot's heart sank. All she wanted was for her girls to be happy.

"Oh love, what do you mean you don't fit in?"

"Well, the teacher made us all stand up in turn and say our names, what school we'd come from, and where we lived."

"Well I'm sure there were other children from your old school, weren't there?"

"Not in my class, Mum. They've split us all up. Some of us are in the two grammar stream classes, some in parallel and some in secondary. None of my friends are in my group."

Despite her daughter's distress, Dot was secretly pleased. Ann had made it into the grammar stream group. That was wonderful news.

"Oh love, I'm sure it'll be okay once you get used to it. It's always a bit hard making new friends. Just be yourself. They'll all love you once they get to know you."

A few weeks later, Ann came home in tears again.

"But Mum, a few of them were really horrible to me at breaktime. They asked where I got my uniform from—said it looked secondhand, not good quality like theirs, so obviously it didn't come from Lester Bowden's. I said we got my blazer, hat, and tie from there. They were really horrible about my raincoat.

*When I came back from lunch it was raining, so they were all in the classroom waiting for the teacher, and one girl was wiping the chalk off the blackboard using my folded-up raincoat, saying that was 'all it was fit for.' And I heard a couple of the girls pointing to our house and talking about how I was '**one of them, the kids they weren't supposed to talk to. The ones who live on the council estate.**'"*

Dot's heart broke for her precious girl. She wanted to march over to the school and give those horrible girls a piece of her mind. How dare they treat Ann like that, just because she came from a poorer home than they did?

"Oh, love. They shouldn't have done that, that was so unkind. You are just as good as the rest of them, much better, probably. Please try not to be so upset. One day, you'll show them. One day, they'll be sorry they ever treated you so badly."

She hugged her girl tightly, trying to dry both their tears with her small cotton handkerchief. At the same time, Dot thought back to when she herself was young, after her own mum had died and she had gone to the Ragged School, and then again after her step-mother had left. Both times, she had been teased and bullied by the other kids. She had hated it then, and now her beloved daughter was going through the same agonies, just because they were poor. She remembered that awful day when Ann had been about nine or ten years old and had come home from Sunday School in tears.

"Oh love, whatever's wrong?"

"Linda says I'm not allowed to go to her party."

"But you were supposed to be going there straight after Sunday School."

"I know, but she lined us all up in the playground after Sunday School and asked what present we were taking to her party. I had to say I wasn't taking anything, as we couldn't afford it. She said I couldn't go, then."

She started sobbing again.

Dot was so incensed that she had gone straight to the kitchen cupboard and taken out a two shilling piece that she had been saving to put in the gas meter.

"Ben, will you please go 'round to the shop and buy a box of Maltesers? Ann can take those to the party. I'm not having anyone treat our girl like that."

Without a word, Ben got on his bike to do as she asked. His face was white. He was so angry that someone had treated his precious daughter so badly.

By the time he got back from the shop, Linda and her mother were standing on their doorstep.

"I am so sorry. I asked Linda why Ann hadn't arrived with all the other children and she told me what she'd said. She's come to apologise."

She had then insisted that Ann–and the box of Maltesers that Dot had angrily thrust into little Linda's hands–walked back to the party with them. Ann pretended to have a good time, joining in all the games, but she couldn't wait to go home as soon as her dad turned up to collect her.

Dot had wanted so much to make it better. To stop her daughters from having embarrassing, heartbreaking moments like that, just because they were poor. Obviously at the moment, she couldn't change their financial circumstances, but maybe some good news would help.

"Guess what Ann? We're going to have another baby."

"Oh Mum, that's so lovely. I do hope it will be another girl. I love having sisters."

Dot smiled weakly, glad that she had given Ann something to smile about. But for herself, she was devastated.

At the age of 41, she had imagined her childbearing days were over. Her youngest was now six by this time and had just started school, so at last, Dot had a little more time to herself. She was still doing her little sewing jobs, and six months ago she had answered an advert in the local paper asking for a cleaning lady. Now, three times a week, after dropping the girls at school, she walked to Epsom Downs, where she spent four hours each time cleaning a house. It was a big, beautiful house right opposite the racecourse, and it was owned by a lovely couple. The Crosslands were a retired business couple, and the house was full of beautiful antiques. The elderly pair quickly took Dot under their wing, realising that, although she might have been reduced to cleaning houses to supplement her family's income, there was actually much more to this shy young woman. They asked about her husband, her children, and her life. They soon learnt that she was very intelligent and interested in all that was going on in the world around her. Dot was well read and informed about the latest world news. They were saddened to hear that she couldn't fulfill all her dreams–especially because they had a daughter of their own. She was a lovely, albeit rather indulged girl who had been to an expensive boarding school, wore designer dresses, and was training to be a nurse in the hopes of securing a rich surgeon husband. While the couple loved their daughter dearly, they realised how lucky she had been to have so many opportunities to pursue her dreams–whilst Dot was having to squash her own ambitions to provide for her little family.

It had taken Dot a few months to realise she was pregnant for a fourth time.

At her age, she had just assumed her body was going through "the change"–that old-fashioned way of describing menopause. Obviously, the contraception they had given her at the family planning clinic had not worked. She would never trust that cervical cap thing again! She had heard about a new contraceptive pill, something that supposedly promised young women a brighter future–a future free from the constant worry of unwanted pregnancies. It was now 1962, so perhaps at last, women would be free to choose their paths.

By the time she was certain, it was too late. She would not ever have considered a termination, but at her age, another pregnancy was risky.

Another baby. Her heart sank just thinking about it. Whatever would Ben say?

"Oh love, I wasn't expecting that."

"Oh, and I suppose you think I'm happy about it, do you?"

"Of course not, love. But we'll manage. We always do."

"Oh Ben. Just when things were getting better. Just when I thought we'd turned a corner at last. What with your pay rise and my new little cleaning job. I thought things were finally going our way. And now this."

She burst into tears. Tears of anger, frustration, and disappointment.

A few weeks after this, she told Ann. She hadn't intended to tell anyone for months, certainly not until her bump started to show. It was a bit embarrassing, having another baby at her age. Whatever would people think? She had only told Ann to cheer the girl up. Now she wished she hadn't done it. Ann was already going around telling everyone that they were going to have another baby. She had even borrowed some wool from Dot's knitting bag and started trying to knit some baby booties.

She knew it was time to tell her employers. The last thing they would want was to have a heavily pregnant cleaning lady.

"Oh Dot, how thrilling! Another baby. I wish I could have had more than one. It just never seemed to happen after we had our Wendy. Both of us would have loved more children. Now, let's be practical. You must take care of yourself. When's the baby due? December, how lovely, a baby in time for Christmas. Well, you must stop working as soon as it's getting too much. I do worry about you walking all the way here. I might get Mr. Crossland to pick you up and drop you home every day. Shame I never learnt to drive, but I know he won't mind. We've both become very fond of you. And of course, you must come back to work just as soon as you feel up to it–bring the baby with you! We can put the pram outside in the garden on sunny days."

Dot was overjoyed. She had never expected this response– never expected her new employers to be so kind to her.

Despite having many months at her disposal, Ann never managed to finish knitting those little booties. She was not a very proficient knitter, despite her mum's guidance. Ann was rather too impatient, dropping stitches constantly. By the time the baby arrived, she had only achieved one rather misshapen piece of knitting, certainly nothing suitable for a newborn baby's delicate little foot.

Her little sister, Margaret, the final child in the family, was born at home on a Thursday afternoon, while the girls were downstairs watching Crackerjack! on the little black and white television set. Ben had been pacing outside in the garden. How he wished that Dot had done as the doctor had suggested and had this baby in hospital. But he knew better than to try and change his wife's mind. Her first hospital birth with little Ann had left indelible scars. It was better that she gave birth at home, where she felt safe. Still, he just wished it would be over. He hated to think of her suffering. Of course, there would be no loud screaming, that's why she'd been happy to keep the girls at home. She knew she could labour quietly; she certainly wasn't going to do anything to upset her precious daughters.

"Okay, you can all come upstairs now to see your little sister. Quiet though, your mum's a bit tired and she doesn't want you making too much noise. Dad, you come too. Well, come on then! Chop, chop."

The midwife spoke sharply, but only because she was tired. She had been up all night delivering another baby, and although Dot's hadn't taken too long, it had made her a bit sad watching the tired mother try not to make a fuss, not to scream out every time she had a strong contraction. What a brave young woman she was.

"Oh Dad, isn't she beautiful? Aren't we lucky to have another sister?"

"Do you think she'll like her pram? I hope she likes the colour!"

As this pregnancy had not been planned, Dot and Ben had parted with all their baby things years ago. They had got rid of the pram, the cot, and all the tiny clothes used by their first three children. Now that Margaret was here, they were forced to replace everything. There was no money to buy shiny new things, but a neighbour had kindly lent them a cot, and Dot had been busily knitting and sewing tiny clothes for the baby. Of course, they had no idea whether it would be a boy or a girl, so she just used pastel colours.

Ben had spotted an advert in the local paper for a pram. By this time, Dot couldn't really care less what the pram looked like, she just wanted to get the baby safely delivered. It had been a difficult pregnancy; she had been sick nearly every day, not just in the mornings, but all day and most evenings too. It had been such a miserable time. She almost felt as though this little one knew it wasn't really wanted. She seemed to spend half her time in tears, worrying about how they would cope.

"Dad, can I come with you to collect the pram? I can push it home, it will be good practice!"

Ben smiled down at Ann. She was such a sweet girl.

"Oh love, it's a long walk all the way to Tattenham Corner and back."

"Oh please, Dad. I promise I'll be good. And I won't moan about being tired."

It was dark when they set off, but luckily the rain held off. When they reached the housing estate, Ann started counting off the house numbers... 23, 25, 27, 29.

"Oh look Dad, it's that one. The one with the hall light on."

The pram was in pretty good condition, although Ben wasn't sure what Dot would say about the colour. Although they didn't have much money, she was always pretty particular, making sure the girls were well dressed. They were never in anything too flashy.

"I'll tell you what, love. Why don't we stop at the off-licence and buy your mum some cider? And maybe some crisps for you and your sisters?"

During this pregnancy, Dot, who had been a teetotaller for pretty much all her life, had suddenly developed a craving for cider. Ben had tried to buy her the occasional bottle whenever he could.

"Oh Dad, can we really? Have we got enough money?"

It broke his heart hearing this from his daughter. He hated how Ann was so aware of how poor they were, how they could never afford new clothes or holidays like her friends, how they couldn't afford to buy a car, a fridge, or even a television. They rented theirs from Radio Rentals, which seemed a bit ironic, given he had all those old sets in the shed that just needed a bit of tinkering with. One day he would get round to mending them. He was quite capable, had all the knowledge and most of the parts to fix them, but somehow, he never seemed to have the time. He knew it drove Dot mad. He longed to give his precious girls everything they wanted, everything they deserved. But on his wages, it just wasn't possible.

"Yes, it's okay love. That nice lady let us have the pram a bit cheaper than expected, so there's enough left over to buy a few treats."

Ann was thrilled. Pushing the big, heavy pram up the hill towards home, she knew she would always remember that day–the day when she and her dad bought the baby's pram and filled it with cider and crisps to take home.

After the girls had gone to bed, Dot sat on the old sofa, her swollen feet resting on a cushion. She was sipping a glass of cider.

"Oh Ben, thank you. It's a lovely pram, in pretty good condition and so sturdy. It's just like the ones the royal family have, big and upright. But I'm not so sure about the maroon colour."

THE CHILDHOOD YEARS

The next few years passed quickly. Far too quickly.

It seemed like no time had passed since baby Margaret was born, and before they knew it, their eldest, Ann, announced she was leaving home. Leaving home to get married.

She was only 19, and Dot was devastated. In a way, it would have been easier to cope if Ann was marrying her first boyfriend, Paul, a lovely young man whom she had known since she was sixteen. Paul was a young man who had become part of the family and was loved by all of them. But sadly, Ann's romance with him only lasted 18 months before she found out he had been seeing another girl. Although she was heartbroken, she told him it was over and that he must never darken her door again.

There had been a few casual boyfriends after that, nice enough young men, but obviously no-one could match her first love. Dot had been relieved; her girl was far too young to think of settling down. She needed to experience more of life, perhaps travel and see the world, discover what she really wanted to do with her time. Dot did not want Ann to just settle for an easy life, a life of boredom and mediocrity. She found that so many women seemed to do that. Thank goodness her girl had a few dreams. How many times had she seen her getting all glazy eyed while she was looking at the Reader's Digest atlas? That had turned out to be such a good buy. She remembered how Ben had been horrified when she first suggested it, when Ann was 11 years old.

"Oh Dot, you know we can't afford it. They can always walk to the library to learn stuff when they need to. We don't need to waste all that money getting our own atlas. Or, if you're adamant, I bet we could find a smaller, cheaper one in the second-hand shop."

For once, Dot had stuck to her guns. This was important to her. She wanted her girls to have every possible chance to better themselves, to experience all the things she had always longed to experience. To travel, to see the world, to learn new things.

"Mum. Can I get out the atlas?"

"Yes, of course, love. As long as you wash your hands first."

She knew she didn't have to tell Ann to be careful with it. The girl treated that book as though it were the crown jewel, turning each page over so carefully, always making sure each shiny sheet was perfectly smooth.

"Mum, have you ever been to Mexico? Did you know that there are crocodiles in the River Nile in Egypt? I wish I could go and see the mountains in Switzerland, just like in my Heidi book."

Dot would smile. She was thrilled that Ann was so like her, fascinated by the world and eager to learn about other people, places, and things. Hopefully, her girl would have the chance to experience more than she had ever managed to. She was certainly determined that Ann would have a more fulfilling life–the kind of life she herself had always dreamt of. In fact, she still dreamt of having it. Ben had an inquisitive mind too; he was always going to the library, finding new things to be passionate about.

"Weren't they lovely chocolates Mrs. Crossland sent us, Mum?"

Dot nodded.

"I'm going to keep all the lovely wrappers. I've told the others they mustn't throw theirs away; I want to keep them all and put them in my scrapbook. One day, I want to visit all those places."

Mrs. Crossland, the lady Dot cleaned for, had just sent them an enormous box of Swiss chocolates–all the way from Lausanne in Switzerland, where they were currently staying with a millionaire friend on holiday. The chocolates had come in an enormous square box, each individual piece wrapped in shiny gold paper with another wrapper on top depicting a colourful Swiss scene. Ann had counted, all 48 chocolates had a different picture.

Over the years, the Crosslands had proved to be a wonderful addition to Dot's life. Although she was only their cleaning lady, they treated her with great respect. They were always trying to ensure she was well and happy. Despite the fact that they were wealthy, they never made her feel inferior and were always marvelous to her children. During the school holidays, knowing that Dot had no one to care for them, Mrs. Crossland insisted that she bring all the girls to work with her. Dot was always anxious about this—the house was full of lovely furniture and beautiful antiques. But somehow, in that environment, her children thrived. They behaved beautifully each time, never letting their mother down, and thus were considered to be *"beautiful, well-mannered children."* Dot knew that some of her employer's wealthy friends did not approve of the situation. She could imagine their questions: *"Why on earth would the Crosslands allow a bunch of council house kids into their home? Surely, they could find a childless cleaner?"*

The kindness Dot's children received there began a legacy. Young Ann, aged eleven at the time and discovering that being a poor council house kid was considered shameful, vowed that when she was grown up, she would be a fine lady like Mrs. Crossland. She planned to always treat everyone with kindness and dignity, regardless of their background.

Those childhood years seem to pass so quickly. There had been lots of awful times—truly awful times—like Ben's illness and Dot's foot operation, which had gone so horribly wrong that she could no longer wear nice shoes. At the age of just 34, she had to resort to old-fashioned, old ladies' shoes for the rest of her life. Then there had been 14-year-old Ann's emergency appendix operation and all the worry that entailed. Little Carol, at the age of five, had toppled down the stairs and was concussed for three whole weeks. Ben had numerous accidents, like falling off his bike on the icy roads, almost cutting his ear off on the tiled fireplace and losing a huge amount of blood. There were constant burst pipes every winter, which meant the house was full of buckets to stop the drips. After some time, Ben developed severe asthma and bronchitis—so severe that he had to resign from his job at Philips. Apparently, the fumes from the new colour televisions they were manufacturing were harmful to him, so he went to work for one of their subsidiary companies. It was closer to home, but for less pay. Dot was convinced that the pipe he had lately taken to smoking was also adding to his health problems, but he was adamant.

"Don't be silly, love. Pipe smoking is very healthy, even better than cigarettes, which they say are good for clearing the lungs. They reckon that the coke and coal we burn on our fires does us all more harm than smoking does. Look at my old dad and grandad—they both smoked all their lives and they're pretty healthy. It's 1962, science has come a long way. They'd certainly know if it wasn't good for us by now. Anyway, I only smoke the good stuff. St. Bruno's is my favourite... You can always get me a tin of it for my birthday if you like!"

Dot merely raised her eyebrows. She wasn't sure if he was right. She listened to the news and read all the papers, and she knew that scientists were beginning to question the dangers of smoking.

"While we're on the subject of smoking, when are you going to clear all those tins and jars full of your electrical stuff out of my kitchen cupboards? I'm fed up seeing them there."

"Oh Dot, don't nag. There was plenty of space in there and it's getting a bit crowded in my shed. Anyway, you're not using those shelves for anything else."

She was so angry she couldn't reply for a few minutes.

"Oh Ben. You know if I could afford to, I'd fill those shelves with tins of food and jars of jams and pickles. There's just never enough money left at the end of the week to buy anything except a few essentials. And then you waste money on more nails, screws, and other whatnots you don't even use. I'm really fed up. Sometimes I wonder: What is the point of it all? I don't see how anything is ever going to change. I'm fed up with never having enough to buy everything we need, to give our girls what they need."

She burst into tears.

Taking her in his arms, Ben let her cry for a while, then said, *"Look, love. I'll take the girls out for a bit to give you a break. Maybe we'll go over to Burgh Heath, and they can see the animals in the pet shop."*

While they were gone, Dot did as she always did. Tidied the house, made the beds, then sat on the settee and got out the old tin box–the black box that held so many memories. One by one, she took out the pictures, tears running down her cheeks. Her old army photos made her cry the most, looking at that young face, so full of hope and optimism. As a younger woman, she had been so certain that her future life was going to be golden–a time of fun, fabulous travel and wonderful experiences. Well, she had achieved the love; Ben and her girls were her world. Often they managed to have fun despite not having much money, but sadly, the travel and wonderful experiences had eluded her. That was why she was so desperate for Ann not to rush into marriage too early. She wanted her to experience some things first, to see something of the world, to live a life less ordinary. She knew that a Yugoslavia trip a few years ago had opened her daughter's eyes, but she had really hoped to open them more. Now her precious girl was threatening to get married while she was still a child–19 years old. She was a smart, feisty girl who thought she knew everything.

The Yugoslavia trip had come about by chance. One day, Ann had come home from school looking a bit wistful. Dot knew her daughter so well. She knew that Ann would always try to protect her mum. It had been years since she had spoken about any bullying at school. Any cruel words were kept to herself these days, as she knew her mum and dad could not produce money out of thin air. They could not just conjure up cash so she could compete with her affluent friends, could not suddenly transform their lives so that she wasn't just *"the girl from the council estate."*

"Oh, it's nothing, Mum. I'm fine."

Her 15-year-old daughter always blushed when she was uncomfortable or telling a fib.

"Come on, love. Tell me what's up."

"Oh Mum, I don't want to go anyway."

"Go where?"

Dot knew her girl had been really upset last year when they couldn't afford for her to go on the school ski trip with all her friends.

"Yugoslavia."

"Well, how much does it cost?"

"It doesn't matter, Mum, it's too expensive. We can't afford it."

"Well actually, love, the insurance man was here today. I took a little policy out when you were born, and it's going to mature next month.

Maybe, if there's enough money, we could use that to pay for it."

That evening, she waited until the girls were in bed before she mentioned it to her husband.

"Oh Ben, you should have seen how excited she was. I know you think we should have used that money for something else, but I'm so glad we didn't. That trip is going to change her life. Just you mark my words."

Dot was right. Ann came back from the school trip all bright-eyed and bushy-tailed, talking non-stop about all the wonderful places she had been–places that had come alive from the atlas. She talked about all the places she intended to visit next, just as soon as she could afford it.

And now, just four years later, the same girl was going to throw away all those dreams, just to get married to a boy Dot didn't even like very much. A boy who, however charming he appeared, was just not the right one for her girl.

But of course, it proved impossible to change Ann's mind. The determination and independence that Dot had always so admired in her eldest daughter was now taking her off in quite the wrong direction. As much as she tried to be happy for her girl, Dot was heartbroken. Even Ben expressed his doubts.

"Oh Dot, she's so young, and pretty unworldly and naïve. She thinks she knows everything, but she's so trusting. We've never really told her how cruel and unforgiving the world can be. Maybe that's our fault, maybe we've cushioned her too much?"

They were both quiet for a while, thinking about all the years that had gone by, all the times they might have done things differently.

"Oh, Ben. She's always been her own person. Do you re-member that note she gave us on our wedding anniversary, years ago? Hang on, it's in here, I think."

She fished under the table and brought out the old tin box. She searched through piles of old photos before produc-ing a single, flimsy sheet of paper. Old cream paper, obviously torn from a notebook.

"Dear Mummy and Daddy,

*We're all dreadfully sorry that we couldn't buy you anything for your wedding anniversary, but we hope to buy something later on when we've got more money **and we're allowed out.** Anyway, we hope that you both like your card.*

Your ever-loving children,
Ann, Carol, Joanna, and Margaret xxxxxxx"

By the time Dot and Ben finished laughing, they both felt better. Their beloved, feisty daughter, telling them off even while wishing them a happy anniversary. Hopefully, that strength of character would help her to cope with whatever life threw at her in the future.

At the wedding service, held in the old stone church at Burgh Heath, Dot wept. Ann looked so beautiful in her long, white, satin wedding dress, the dress she had designed herself and got her mum to help her sew. The other girls–her younger sisters and a couple of friends–looked lovely too. Three of them were wearing dresses of yellow satin, the others were wearing orange. It was a very colourful wedding.

Ben knew that Dot was trying to control her tears.

"Dearly beloved, we are gathered here today to celebrate the marriage of Ann and Peter."

"To join this man and this woman in holy matrimony..."

Dot wanted to leap up, to stop it from happening.

"No, no, you're wrong," she wanted to shout. *"She's not a woman, she's just my little girl."*

But of course, she said nothing. In later years, she wondered if things would have turned out better for Ann if she *had* been brave enough to speak up more, to say what a mistake she thought it was. Maybe she could have saved her girl from years of heartache.

1999. APPROACHING THE NEW MILLENNIUM.

Sometimes Dot couldn't believe she had lived so long–that despite everything, she and Ben were still married. They still loved each other.

She was 78 and he 77, and they had weathered so many storms together.

Dot looked over to where Ben was snoozing in his armchair. That's all he seemed to do these days: sleep or eat. She could never manage to get a decent conversation out of him.

She looked around the room, feeling her annoyance rise.

"Ben. Wake up."

"Yes, love? I wasn't really asleep, just resting my eyes."

"I wish we could have a decent conversation sometimes. It's so boring just sitting here listening to your snoring."

"I don't snore."

"Yes, you do; you're loud enough to wake up the whole street. Good job we haven't got the windows open."

Ben wished he could keep his eyes shut. He thought at least by pretending to be asleep, he could escape her constant nagging. But she knew him too well. They had been together for more than 50 years–she thought she knew everything about him.

"Looking 'round this house makes me very fed up, Ben. How many times over the years have I asked you to redecorate the place? It looks so shabby now. I'm ashamed to have anyone visit."

He refrained from saying that, apart from family, hardly anyone did visit. He would have loved to always have a house full of people, a place where friends could congregate and socialise. But Dot had never been much of a socialiser. In that respect, she was very different from him.

"It was okay at the other house 'cos the council used to redecorate it every few years, but now, with all this cost cutting, they don't even bother to come and do anything. We tenants are just supposed to do it all ourselves. It's okay if you have a handyman in the family... or a husband who likes decorating. I wonder if you'd have been any different if we owned the house instead of just renting it?

I wish we could have afforded to buy one. But I guess, like other things in life, it was just not meant to be."

She sighed dramatically and Ben raised his eyebrows. Here we go again. Like a broken record, a catalogue of all his failings.

"Ben, are you listening? Don't pretend you can't hear me."

He closed his eyes again as she droned on. He loved her dearly, but just wished she could let it all go, all the frustration and anger. She was full of anger and disappointment because her life hadn't turned out as she had hoped. She had so many regrets.

He had tried so hard to be a good husband. Of course their life hadn't been easy, it was not particularly rosy, but at least they had been blessed with a lovely little family. Their girls had all grown up into fine young women–women he was really proud to call his daughters–and now there were the grandchildren, too. All such lovely little things, four girls and two boys. He smiled as he thought of each of them, his precious little ones. Of course, they weren't so little anymore; the eldest grandchild was 14 and the youngest 4.

"Ben, why don't you answer when I talk to you? I might as well just talk to myself for all the conversation I get from you. I know you chat to everyone when you go out. Mrs. Cross from next door told me she met you in the supermarket the other day, and you chatted for twenty minutes. I guess maybe I'm just not exciting enough for you."

He looked across at his wife as she sat in the armchair opposite him. She had taken off her reading glasses and was staring at him, accusingly.

He made the fatal mistake of laughing, which just incensed her more.

"Don't you dare laugh at me, Ben. I'm not joking." She sounded close to tears.

Reluctantly, he got up from his chair. Every part of his old body ached, but he needed to hold her.

"Oh, Squibs."

She was shocked. It had been years since he called her by their nickname.

"Please don't cry. I love you, you know I do. I'm just not very good at showing it. But I do try to be a good husband."

As he held her tightly in his arms, it felt as though all the years had melted away and they were young again, on their honeymoon in Torquay. A time of love, passion, and hopes for the future. Big dreams. Sadly, many of those dreams had not come true.

They had been lucky enough to make a lovely family, and until now, they had all been in reasonably good health. But they had never seemed to thrive financially. Like many young couples after the war, they had to live with Ben's parents for a few years until they were lucky enough to get a council house to rent. They had always hoped to save enough money to buy their own place one day, and actually, they had almost done it. Years ago, when Maggie Thatcher decided to sell off a lot of the government housing stock, sitting tenants like them were offered their homes at bargain prices. Ben and Dot had gone to the bank and been offered a mortgage. Just when they were about to complete their purchase, Ben was suddenly made redundant. It had been such a blow–one that Dot had never really recovered from. He hadn't minded so much, he was just trying to get the house for her really, but in the twenty years since then, Ben had noticed that she often brought it up as another of his failings.

She didn't really like the house, so he had always been a bit surprised at how disappointed she was by not being able to buy it. Of course, they were allowed to stay there–renting it for the rest of their lives–but he knew how she hated to hear about all their neighbours investing money and time on their "newly-purchased" homes.

It became a big issue for them. Maybe he *would* have been more inclined to look after and decorate the house better if he *had* actually owned it. However, now, at the age of 77, all he wanted was a quiet life–a life where he could go for a nice bike ride or walk to the shops or the library. He sought a life where he could get up, have a leisurely breakfast, read a book, watch a bit of television, play with his grandchildren, and relax. Maybe have an afternoon nap every now and then.

"And sometimes I wish we'd never moved to this house. I know it's only 'round the corner from our old one, but it's so different. I liked living on that cul-de-sac where we knew everyone."

He sunk back into his chair. Obviously she had a lot to say, so he might as well get comfortable.

"Do you remember that nice wallpaper we had in the hallway? Trailing freesias on a cream background. I loved that pattern. I used to love seeing it when I was sitting on the stairs, looking out the window. It must have cost a fortune for the council to distribute all those big heavy wallpaper catalogues so we could choose our own paper."

He chuckled.

"Why are you laughing at me?"

"Oh love, I'm not laughing at you. Just remembering how you always used to moan about not having big picture windows in the old house, yet now, when we do have a big window looking onto the street, you keep it covered up with a net curtain."

"But it's different, Ben. We used to live on a nice little street where there weren't masses of cars driving up and down. It was much quieter there. Just the occasional car and all the kids playing outside. And the neighbours were all nice and respectable.

Not like some of the sights you see wandering up and down this street!"

Ben chuckled again.

"In the old days, you wouldn't have seen all these young girls walking around in barely any clothes. It must be such a worry to their mothers. I'm glad my girls aren't teenagers anymore."

"Oh Dot, you can't have forgotten how our Ann and her friends used to parade around in their tiny little mini-skirts. I seem to remember that you even shortened your skirts in those days to keep up with the latest fashion!"

He was right. In the late 1960s, she too had succumbed to the latest trends and worn mini-skirts. Even the Queen had shortened her skirts to just above her knee!

She smiled. Funny how talking about all this brought everything back. Her mind was suddenly flooded with memories and images of that time.

"Do you remember how our Ann used to buy material from the market and expect me to sew her a new dress to go to a dance that very night? Cheek of the girl."

"And you always used to do it, drop whatever else you were doing and get out your needle and thread."

"Some of that stuff she brought home was rubbish. Cheap, flimsy muck, so hard to sew."

"But she was always thrilled with the outcome. You always did such a good job. Mind you, you've always been a wonderful tailoress, everyone knows that. Look at all those lovely clothes you made for the kids when they were little. Even when we didn't have any money, you always made sure they were clean and nicely dressed."

"Do you remember the time I cut up that old checked tablecloth and made the girls' sunsuits? We've got a photo of them wearing them in the garden somewhere. Baby Carol was only small. There were only the two of them then. I must fish it out and show the girls next time they're here, they'll be tickled pink."

"I remember all those lovely party dresses you made. You used to buy the material with the money your dad gave them every Christmas. A 10s note and a bar of Cadbury chocolate. That's what he used to give all of us, even us adults. I miss your old dad, he was such a gent."

They were both quiet for a while, remembering Dot's dad, Valentine George. His sudden death, back in 1968, had come as such a shock to them all. Everyone missed his quiet presence.

"Oh Ben. I do miss them all."

Dot had now lost all her family except for her brother John. Everyone else was long gone. Sometimes, she wished she had made more of an effort with Ben's family and allowed his mum and dad more access to the girls. Perhaps she should have swallowed her pride and let Eustace, Lou, and Lou's sisters—Ben's aunties—be part of their family. At least then, her own children would have had plenty of relatives, people they could call their own. She remembered Ben's aunties at their wedding, those five tall, imposing sisters. She had never given them a chance really, had never allowed herself to think of them as her new family. Now that seemed rather silly, a stupid, selfish decision and one that she knew Ben rather resented. He never mentioned it, but she knew that he missed them. His family had always been so close, and in recent years he had only seen his aunties or cousins occasionally, mostly if they had been visiting his mum and dad when he happened to be there too. Now of course, his mum and dad were gone, so he had pretty much lost touch with them all. A whole chunk of his life was lost.

"Do you remember when your Aunty Rose came and lived with us for a while? That was a tricky time, wasn't it?"

Dot's beloved Aunty Rose, the heroine of her younger years, had been in her eighties then. She had been widowed several years earlier, and was lost without her husband, Cyril. He had been her absolute rock for so many years. He had allowed her to be herself–a free spirit–and had loved her absolutely. Without him, she was bereft. After his death, she quickly sold the family home in Edgware, finding it too sad and empty without her husband or her mum Martha, who had lived with them until she died. Her son Douglas had been furious. She had not consulted him before putting the house on the market, so in his view, she had sold it far too cheaply, making a dent in his inheritance. From there, she moved to the seaside, buying a nice little house right on the seafront, but she soon tired of that. After a couple of years, she moved again to a pretty little country cottage in a Sussex village. It was a lovely chocolate box cottage with a thatched roof, a little back garden, and roses around the door.

Each time, she moved hastily, ignoring all advice. Living life as she had always done–on her own terms.

One day, she turned up unannounced at Dot's house, carrying a big carpet bag over her arm. She looked exhausted, having travelled by train, two buses, and a long walk from the nearest bus stop. Dot offered her tea and was about to make it really strong, just as Rose had always liked, when the older woman stopped her.

She produced a tin from her copious handbag. *"Peppermint tea. It's the only thing I drink these days, my dear, due to my digestion. Although sometimes, I do have a bit of ginger. That helps too.*

Anyway Dot, I thought I'd come and stay a few weeks, if you don't mind. I'm putting my house on the market and I've told the agent to let it go for whatever he can get. I can't go back there—not with that madman living next door."

Dot was stunned. It was only a couple of months before that they had all gone down to visit her. They had loved her little house and met her neighbour, an elderly gentleman in his eighties who was obviously delighted that such a vibrant woman had come to live next door.

"He stands in my garden in the middle of the night, just staring in through my windows. I tell him to go away, but he comes back every night. I just can't stand it anymore, so I've got to move. You don't mind if I stay here with you lot until I find another place to buy, do you? I'd quite like to be nearer to you all. I don't know why I moved so far away in the first place. You're all the family I've got left now, you and my brother Valentine. It seems silly not to spend my last few years living closer to everyone."

Dot had been thrilled. She loved her aunt; she was the closest thing to a mother she had had since she was 13. If she had her way, she would have invited Rose to live with them forever, but it just wasn't possible. Their house was so small. It only had two bedrooms, and all the children were squashed into one, while she and Ben had the other. They did have a put-you-up in the living room, so if they moved that into the little dining area, they could make up the folding bed and Rose could have her own private space. It would only be for a few weeks, after all.

It was a happy time. The children loved Rose and she made such a fuss of them. Valentine George even made one of his rare visits so that he could catch up with his sister.

"Dot, do you think Rose is okay? She seems to be acting a bit strange to me."

"Oh Dad, don't make a fuss. You know she's always been a bit eccentric, that's why we all love her so much."

"I know, love. That sister of mine has never really conformed to anything, but I am a bit worried about her. She doesn't seem to have been able to settle anywhere since she lost Cyril. He was such a good husband to her. Don't know how he put up with her sometimes. By the way, have you heard from Douglas? He doesn't seem to take much notice of what his mum's up to... unless he wants something. And that wife of his is such a snob, thinks we're all a bit beneath her, I think."

Dot thought about this conversation as she was walking home after seeing her dad off at the bus stop that day. He was right. Rose did seem to be behaving a bit oddly, but surely it was just the grief. So much upheaval and sadness. She just needed to find somewhere nice to settle down. What a shame she couldn't live with them permanently. They all loved having her around, there just wasn't enough room for it to work long term—especially now that the kids were growing up so fast.

"Mum, there's a police car outside."

Dot groaned. Rose had taken to going out for a little stroll in the mornings, and instead of coming home in time for lunch as planned, she often decided to hop on the bus and go for an adventure. This was the third time in a fortnight she had gone missing.

"Oh, Aunty Rose. Whatever happened?"

"Well, love, I was just walking past the bus stop and saw the 164 bus coming, so I decided to hop on it. I haven't been to Sutton in ages. I had a nice time wandering around the shops, but then it started getting late and I couldn't remember how to get home. So I found a nice policeman and they kindly gave me a lift."

She began to wander farther afield, each time arriving home in a police car rather late and rather dishevelled.

Dot became increasingly worried and phoned her dad. Valentine said that he would ring Douglas, Rose's only child. It was about time the man took some responsibility for his mother after all she had done for him.

A few days later, he turned up at the house.

"Hello Dot, how are you? I've come for Mother. She will be better off living with us. I can keep an eye on her there."

Rose was crying when he dragged her out the front door half an hour later. He was impatient to get back to his big house in North London; he had a dinner appointment at his country club and was looking forward to a nice steak.

"But I don't understand why I can't stay here with Dot and the children. I won't be any trouble. You like having me around, don't you Dot?"

Dot was too choked up to speak properly. The children were watching, open mouthed, unsure why this strange man was being allowed to kidnap their great aunt.

"We'll see you soon, Aunty, I promise. Douglas, you will bring her to see us, won't you? Or we could come up on the train and visit her at your place!"

He was too busy shoving his elderly mother into the car to reply. He locked the passenger door of the shiny BMW so that she couldn't escape, and nodded his head in farewell. Dot could see her aunt frantically banging on the car window as she was driven away.

It was six months before they saw Rose again. Douglas ignored all Dot's pleas, refusing to bring his mother to visit them. In addition, every date Dot suggested was apparently "unsuitable" for the family to come to North London. She began to think she would never see her aunt again. She wrote several letters, but they remained unanswered; she was not sure whether Rose ever even received them.

One afternoon, there was a frantic knocking on the front door. Dot was alone in the house, Ben and Ann were at work, and the younger children were still at school.

"Oh thank God you're here. I thought you'd moved away. I thought I'd never see you again. I've been so miserable. Why didn't you ever bother to come and see me?"

Dot hardly recognised the bedraggled creature standing in front of her. If it hadn't been for the familiar old carpet bag hanging from her arm, she would have not known her aunt at all.

Rose had lost so much weight. She had always been a very attractive, vibrant lady–a lady who would turn heads wherever she went—but now, she looked like a tramp. A grubby old woman, with shabby clothes and a sad, wild-eyed appearance.

"*Oh Aunty, whatever's happened? I thought you were safe at Douglas's place?*"

"*I'm never going back there, not if they drag me. I'd rather die than live with that lot. Treated me like I was something the cat brought in. I've always known he was ashamed of me. A poor old lady who's not good enough to mix with all his posh friends... Good enough to provide him with money though! He's made sure that all the money from my house sale went into his investments and said I was incapable of managing my own affairs any longer. Said I was losing my mind, going senile.*"

"*Oh, Aunty.*"

"*I waited 'til they'd all gone to work, then I sneaked out. Got the Tube to Victoria, then the train to Morden, and the bus all the way here. I couldn't believe it when I finally got to your house, exhausted and dying for a cuppa—only to be told you'd moved. The lady in your old house didn't seem to know where you'd gone and I was getting a bit het up, but then your old neighbour, that one whose husband works as a printer on Fleet Street, came home and told me you'd only moved 'round the corner. She was even kind enough to walk around here with me, to make sure I got to the right place.*"

"*But didn't you get all my letters? I've written four or five to you, and of course I told you we were moving—even sent you our new address.*

I did think it was a bit funny that you didn't reply, but I thought perhaps you were cross with me for letting Douglas take you away."

Rose reached across and gave Dot's hand a squeeze.

"*Oh, love, I really couldn't bear to think you had forgotten about me, but when I didn't hear from you I just feared the worst. Feared that you had chucked your old aunty on the scrapheap and forgotten all about me. It did break my heart.*"

It took a while for them both to calm down. After two cups of strong tea, they felt better.

"*The council said we were overcrowded in that little house, so they offered us this one instead. I didn't really want to move, but Ben said it would be more comfy having more space now that the girls are growing up. This place has three bedrooms and a separate toilet, so at least we aren't all queuing up to use the loo every morning while someone's having a wash! Mind you, I miss the old place. So many memories there. We were there for 13 years, you know.*"

"*Do you think I could stay with you all for a few days, just 'til I find my feet?*"

Of course, they welcomed her once again with open arms. They had all missed her. The girls loved listening to all her stories about growing up in London.

"*Mum, did you know that Aunty Rose was already born when Queen Victoria was still alive?*"

"*Mum, did you know that Aunty Rose used to be a waitress at Lyons Corner House? She worked in the West End and said she often used to serve famous people, even film stars!*"

"*Mum, what do you think Aunty Rose keeps in that big bag of hers? She says they're her treasures. Do you think she's really rich?*"

"*Can she live with us forever?*"

They moved the two youngest girls into the little box room that Ben had been using as an office-cum-workshop, and Rose moved in with the older girls. Ann and Carol loved having her there. She would occasionally sneak them toffees from her handbag and they would guiltily eat them, knowing they had already cleaned their teeth and their mum would be cross if she knew.

"Girls, girls. Wake up. I've got something important to tell you."

Ann knew it was late, but definitely not past midnight yet, as she could hear the hum from the television downstairs. Her dad loved staying up late to watch his favourite programmes, but her mum always insisted the TV went off by midnight if not sooner. She always made them laugh by saying that their dad was going to get square eyes one day because he loved the television so much!

"Now, be quiet girls. We don't want your parents to hear."

They were sleepy. Her next words made them think that perhaps they were still sleeping, and this was just a silly dream.

"It's very important that we keep quiet, only talk in whispers. We don't want them to hear us."

Ann was puzzled. It definitely wasn't a dream. It really was Aunty Rose sitting on the edge of her bed. But why was she whispering?

*"I was downstairs just now, watching the news, when **they** came on.*

I knew at once that your parents were in cahoots with them. It was obvious by the way they acted, all furtive like."

The girls looked at each other in confusion. What on earth was she talking about?

*"**Them**–the Russians, of course. I'd suspected for a while that they'd infiltrated this house, but I never imagined your mum and dad would fall for their lies."*

Ann was 17 and understood a little about world affairs. She worked in a bank, and there was always talk at break times. Talk about the state of the world and politics. She had heard of the Cold War, but had certainly never expected it to affect her own life.

"Oh, Aunty Rose, are you sure? I don't think mum or dad would ever side with the Russians."

"Yes, love, I'm very sure. I've heard Russian voices coming through the walls for a few days now, I just can't believe your mum and dad are stupid enough to believe everything they hear. Anyway, we must stay on the alert. Don't discuss this with any-one, especially not your mum and dad, or we'll all be in danger. Go to sleep now, and I'll keep watch. All night if necessary."

Ann barely slept a wink all night. She could hear her sister and Aunty Rose snoring gently in the darkness, along with her dad's loud snoring from the bedroom next door. Usually she found his snoring comforting, but not tonight. She couldn't believe that her lovely dad was on the side of the Russians. Or her mum? But she knew she couldn't ask them about it, or it would put them all in danger.

The next morning, everyone seemed normal at breakfast. It was a Saturday, so neither she, nor her dad had to go to work. She noticed Rose casting the odd, suspicious glance towards her parents, but apart from that, everything seemed just the same as usual.

A couple of days later, after being woken up again in the middle of the night, she plucked up some courage and spoke to her mum. They were alone in the house. Rose had taken the other girls to the sweetshop.

"Mum?"

"Yes, love." Dot was distracted. She was putting the finishing touches to a yellow dress and jacket, an outfit she was making for a young girl who lived on the next street. She was having to let in a few more inches on the waistband, as the lass seemed to have put on a bit of weight since her first fitting a few weeks ago. Dot wasn't surprised. She had guessed the girl was pregnant by the way she sat awkwardly and refused a cup of tea. Such a shame. The girl was only 19 and unmarried. Apparently she had a boyfriend, but he wasn't prepared to marry her until the baby arrived and he was sure it was his. Dot was so angry thinking about this that she pricked herself with the needle several times, almost getting blood on the yellow material. It was now the 1960s, but in reality, nothing much seemed to have changed since Victorian times. Men still had their wicked ways and the poor girls were left to pick up the pieces. It just wasn't fair.

"I need to tell you something, but it's a secret."

Dot's heart sank. Surely her girl wasn't going to say she was pregnant too? That was her worst nightmare. Of course, she realised now that she hadn't been much good at giving advice, hadn't told her about the facts of life and all that, but she just hadn't known how to. Not having a mum or sisters herself, she had just had to learn about the birds and bees as she went along. It would have been too embarrassing trying to explain all that stuff to Ann. But now her daughter had a boy-friend–a nice-enough lad, good looking and intelligent, just a year older than Ann. Certainly not old enough to be a father.

"Mum, are you listening? This is important."

Dot was so relieved to hear that her girl wasn't expect-ing a baby, but she was devastated to hear about the Russian business. She had been wondering herself if Rose was all right lately; she often seemed a bit distant and in a world of her own. Dot had just put it down to Rose's advancing years. After all, she had lived a long and interesting life–always protected by her husband–and now he was gone, leaving her to fend for herself. Her son didn't seem to care much. Dot had rung him to say his mum was safe and staying with them for a while. All the while he had just listened politely, ending the conver-sation with:

"Well, rather you than me. She was driving us all mad here with her constant demands and criticisms. Let me know when you want to get rid of her."

Dot had been furious. How dare he speak about her lovely aunty like that? Even if she was his mum! It just made her more determined to give the old lady a safe and happy home for as long as she possibly could. Of course, it added to the food bill, but she didn't care. Rose had been such a big part of her life, had often stepped in to help the motherless girl. Now the least she could do was return the favour.

"Don't worry, Ann, love. She's just settling in, it's probably all a bit strange to her right now. She's had so much sadness and loss the last few years. We just need to look after her. She'll soon be right as rain again."

In her heart, Dot knew this probably wasn't true, but she really wanted to believe it. Ben was supportive, too. He was very fond of Rose and knew how much Dot loved having her around.

For a few months, it all ticked along nicely. Rose seemed to have forgotten about the Russians, or at least, she never mentioned them. She started going on little adventures again, usually coming back at the appointed time, and occasionally was brought home in a police car after having ventured too far from home.

One day, she came home in tears, wailing that someone had stolen her jewellery.

"Right from my bag they took it, Dot. So brazen they were! I'd only put my bag down for a minute."

A couple of days later, Rose remembered she had taken it into the jewellers in Sutton, exchanging it for a bit of cash.

After that incident, someone always tried to go with her when she insisted on an outing.

"Oh Dot, that would be lovely. We haven't had a nice day out together in ages. Shall we go to the shops, have a bit of lunch, then go to the pictures like we always used to do?"

One day, Ann offered to go with her.

"Oh Mum, it was so awful. We got on the bus and sat on those long seats near the conductor. There was an old man— maybe in his 50s—obviously just going to work, sitting, clutching his lunch box. Aunty Rose glared at him, then insisted we get off the bus. It hadn't even started moving yet I told her we'd have to wait an hour for the next one, but she didn't care. Then, in a loud voice, she announced that he was "one of them, sent to spy

on us." It was so embarrassing; everyone on the bus was staring at us. I couldn't wait to get off. As soon as we did, she calmed down and suggested we pop into the café for a nice cup of tea before we walked home."

Dot was heartbroken. Things began to get worse, and finally, she debated admitting defeat. She just wasn't sure how much longer she could cope. In the end, though, the decision was taken out of her hands. One winter's evening, after the family had eaten dinner and settled down for the evening, there was a loud knock on the door.

"I've come for Mother. It's time she came home. She's been a burden to you for long enough."

He spoke in the clipped, eloquent tone of a man used to giving orders. After an excellent university education–funded entirely by his parents–he got a good job and rose quickly through the ranks. It didn't hurt that he had married the boss's only and much-loved daughter. Of course, his ordinary old mother, whose voice gave away her early, humble upbringing, did not fit into his new life. Whilst his father was still alive, he had managed to avoid seeing too much of them, only visiting his parents occasionally. Ironically, his father, Cyril, one of the nicest men you could ever hope to meet, had been born into an aristocratic family. He had chosen to be disinherited, rather than lose Rose–the love of his life. Cyril had been a gentle, humble person, quite different from the rather pompous man his son had become.

Rose cried and begged to be allowed to stay with Dot's family. The girls clung onto their great aunt, distraught to see her so unhappy. Dot and Ben tried to reason with Douglas, to assure him that they were happy for Rose to stay. They told him she was no trouble and that they all loved having her there.

But he had made up his mind. This had gone on quite long enough; it was time he sorted his mother out once and for all.

Dot's final sighting of her beloved aunt was watching her kick, scream, and try to hit her son with her heavy carpet bag as he shoved her, unceremoniously, into his car. He sped off without a second glance.

A few weeks later, Dot got a brief letter from Douglas.

"Just to let you know, I have found a place for Mother to live. It is about 30 miles from here and quite secure, so at least she won't be able to run away anymore. We couldn't cope with having her here."

She also got a postcard—a plain white one, with not even a pretty picture to soften the blow.

"Dear Dot,

I just wanted to say thank you for all you and Ben have done for me. I'm sure it wasn't always easy; I know how busy you are with all your girls. But I was so happy living with you all. It put some joy back in my life after losing my Cyril. It's a shame his son isn't cut from the same cloth. My Cyril would be turning in his grave if he saw how I've been treated. Anyway, Dot, I don't suppose I'll be seeing you again, so bye for now. Aunty Rose. xx"

Dot wept buckets after receiving this postcard and tried to contact Douglas to get the address of her aunt's new home.

All she knew was that it was a nursing home somewhere within a 30-mile radius of his house.

He never replied, neither to her phone calls nor letters. One day, some six months later, she received this:

"Dot, please don't keep pestering me. It's too late now anyway, as Mother passed away peacefully a couple of months ago. I didn't bother telling you, as I knew you probably couldn't afford the train fare to come to her funeral."

THE FINAL YEARS

The years had gone so fast, much faster than Dot had ever imagined they would. When she was young, she had imagined life would go on forever, that she would never grow old, that everything would always be glorious.

Now she was stuck here, an old lady of 93, living out her final years in this miserable place.

Ninety-three years, an absolute lifetime. How she wished she had enjoyed it more, spent less time fretting about the things she didn't have and more time appreciating the things she did. What a futile waste all that moaning and regret had been. Now, looking back, it seemed so silly. Why on earth hadn't she been able to just relax, live in the moment, and accept that, although things weren't perfect, they were good enough?

Most of all, she regretted the way she had sometimes been too sharp with Ben. She knew she hadn't always been fair to him. She had taken out a lot of her frustrations on him, and to his credit, he had usually allowed her to vent her anger in his direction—letting her talk until her anger subsided. He rarely retaliated, just sunk further into his chair and pretended to go to sleep or announced he was going out on his bike to the supermarket to buy some doughnuts. He loved doughnuts; there were rarely more than a couple left in a box of six by the time he got home. Apparently, he always *"felt a bit peckish cycling home, so thought I'd just try one or two!"* It became a real family joke, Ben and his doughnuts. He had always remained pretty fit and healthy, and even in his late eighties, had ridden his bike whenever possible. In fact, for such an elderly gentleman, he had certainly retained his youthful looks and vigour very well. He remained a very handsome charming man, with many traces of the person Dot had fallen in love with all those years ago.

Over the years, they had both thought about leaving a few times, giving up on a marriage that wasn't really fulfilling either of their dreams. Somehow, though, they had managed to keep it going. Even when times were really hard, when they were in the depths of despair, there had been moments of pure joy. Sometimes they looked at each other over their girls' heads and smiled, knowing that their love and the love they both had for their children was so strong–too strong to let anything destroy it.

Little things brought such joy, like the Friday nights when Ben brought home a few sweets as a treat. He would divide a tube of Smarties–putting the exact same number into four egg cups–or slice up a Mars bar, giving each child exactly the same sized slice. Of course, he always made sure he sampled them too; all his life, Ben had a sweet tooth. Right up until the end of his life, he would often indulge in a bar of Cadbury's Fruit and Nut chocolate, liquorice allsorts, or Pontefract cakes. Luckily for him, his children didn't like liquorice much, so he never had to share those. Sometimes, he would bring Dot one of her favourites, a Nestle Walnut Whip, and the whole family would be content, enjoying their little treats.

There had been plenty of other joyous times, too.

There were the times they went to the Derby and stood with all the crowds at Tattenham Corner as the racehorses thundered past. Afterwards, they crossed over the road to the fairground, where the gypsies sold wooden pegs, lucky heather, or the chance to have one's fortune told. Another time, they had walked along the towpath from Kingston to Hampton Court on a bright, sunny day, stopping to eat fish and chips with their fingers, straight from the newspaper. Sitting beside the River Thames, Ben told his family stories about his young life growing up in Southwark, foraging in the river for treasures. Then there had been their birthdays, when each person had woken up full of excitement to find a trail of birthday cards running from the front door to the living room and leading to a couple of brightly-wrapped presents. Usually, these were things that Dot had stayed up to make, night after night, for her beloved children—perhaps a new dress or some doll clothes, sometimes even a book. For Ben, she usually knitted a jumper or bought him a new tie.

How they had laughed when Dot relayed to Ben the stories of the rag-and-bone man's visit, and how she had allowed the girls to swap some old rags in exchange for a notebook and a dying goldfish. They had both tried so hard to make their girls' lives happy, to give their beloved children memories to treasure even though they had no money.

Neither of them had really been gardeners, but they had tried. They had planted fruit bushes: gooseberries and blackcurrants, and flowers: marigolds, sweet peas, pinks, love-in-a-mist, milkmaids, and ice plants. Ann had grown some hollyhocks, which were pretty, but nothing matched up to the splendour of the next door neighbour's magnificent, prize-winning dahlias. He worked nights in a printing press on Fleet Street, so his garden was a wonderful way for him to relax during the day.

The girls had always been fascinated with the stuff in Ben's shed–the old, broken radios and the piles of wooden-handled tools. When his dad, Eustace, died, Ben inherited all his tools, adding them to his already-vast collection. Occasionally, he would use them, but more often than not, he would just tinker. Ben liked to mend things with his soldering iron or invent a new piece of equipment.

He was always finding new projects, new passions to indulge in. New passions meant more books, which were mostly sourced from second-hand bookshops, so they often had a musty smell. Luckily for Ben, Dot had no sense of smell, otherwise, she might have forbidden him from bringing them into the house!

His wife had been born without a sense of smell, a condition known as congenital anosmia, and over the years, it had been a source of great sadness to her. She had never been able to smell flowers, food, or her babies when they had been bathed and dusted with Johnson's baby powder. Of course, she had never been able to smell bad odours either, which some people thought was a blessing. Her children had never really understood when she had been sad because she could not smell the bluebells they picked for her in the woods or the delicious apple pie she had just taken out of the oven. Because she had never been able to smell anything, she had to just imagine how things smelt. At least she still had a sense of taste, so she was luckier than some.

Ben had always liked that Dot never wore much makeup. He thought she looked beautiful just as she was. A real natural beauty, her kind, caring nature just seemed to shine through. All she had ever used was Nivea cream, a little lipstick, and occasionally a bit of face powder from the pot on her dressing table. Sometimes, Ann and Carol would sneak into her bedroom and open the little blue pot of "Evening in Paris" by Bourjois. They had loved the powder puff inside, as well as the smell of the pastel-coloured dust. Dot could always tell when they'd been in there, as there remained little specks of dust on the floor.

In the old days, during the war and afterwards, when rationing was still in and clothing coupons were hard to get, Dot had used a black pencil to make seams on the back of her legs. This made it look like she was wearing silk stockings. She hadn't bothered to wear make up on her face then, as she was constantly covered in freckles from being outdoors all the time. She wasn't very fond of looking in the mirror–she had never been very confident about her appearance–but she had to admit that the years hadn't been too unkind to her. Her skin was still pretty good, there weren't too many wrinkles, and she'd never bothered to dye her hair. It remained the original mousy brown colour well into her sixties, when a few stray grey hairs began to appear. Ben had kept his youthful looks and magnificent head of hair for a long time, too. Although he had started going bald at the front, his remaining hair was still thick and healthy. In fact, sometimes, when Dot looked across at him snoozing in his armchair, she wanted to get up and stroke his old face–that old, much-loved face that had barely changed since he was the young ex-airman she fell in love with all those years ago. Of course, neither of them were the sprightly young things they had been back in 1948 when they first met; they both had had bits replaced: knees, hips, teeth, and eyes. Arthritis was a constant source of pain for both of them these days, but at least they were still alive–still here to watch their family grow, to help them however they could.

There was so much sadness over the years. In some ways, Dot felt that the lives of her children had been more difficult than her own. There had been divorces–three out of her four children had suffered those. Poor Ann went through it twice, not having chosen either of her husbands very wisely. She was still too trusting, too caring, too forgiving. Only Carol had managed to have a long-lasting marriage, but her tragedy was greater. She lost her only beloved child, Dot and Ben's lovely granddaughter, Yvonne, to a terrible genetic disease. There had been many other deaths, even a couple of suicides. Sometimes, Dot wondered how they had made it through all those dreadful times.

And now, Ben was gone, and she was all alone.

It had happened so suddenly.

He had walked down the road to the fish and chip shop to buy their lunch–a "Friday Pensioner's Special," fish and chips for two for just five pounds! Lately they had been getting lots of takeaways. It was easier than bothering to do a big shop, and neither of them really enjoyed cooking anymore. Well, of course, Ben had never cooked. Like most men of his generation, he had been brought up by an adoring mother who spoiled him, then lovingly looked after by his wife. There had never been any need for him to become domesticated. He knew how to boil an egg if necessary, and certainly would never have starved if he had had to fend for himself, but Dot had always enjoyed caring for her family. After all, she had been running a home since she was 13 years old, since Lizzie left, so feeding people was second nature to her. Sometimes it had been hard, trying to balance the nutritional needs of her husband and children with the few pennies in her purse, but she had always managed to cook nourishing meals. She made lots of stews, often without meat, but always with plenty of other ingredients to fill her children's tummies. Pearl barley, beans, and dumplings were great meat alternatives. When she could afford meat, she always supplemented it with Yorkshire Pudding, crispy roasted potatoes, and lots of vegetables. Sometimes, she made apple or blackcurrant pie, rice pudding, cheese straws, or rock cakes. It was plain, simple cooking, but no one in her house ever went hungry.

Dot smiled to herself, remembering those happy times. How excited the children had been to come home from school and find she had baked some cakes. If only she had realised then how very precious those moments were, but she had always been too busy trying to make ends meet. She was constantly trying to keep her children well fed and happy, making sure they had clean, ironed school uniforms every day and teaching them how to behave. Dot always emphasized doing right from wrong. She taught them to read and love books, that way they could better themselves. She was always busy keeping the house clean and tidy, doing the garden, and working part-time to earn a bit of money and help the family budget. Somehow, in the midst of all that, she had lost herself. She had been so preoccupied with trying to be the perfect mother, the perfect wife, that she had forgotten how to be Dot.

And now, Dot was all she had. Her children were all grown up... even most of her grandchildren were almost adults these days. They all towered over her.

She fidgeted, realising she had been nearly nodding off. That seemed to happen so much now. Her mind would wander here and there. It was funny how stuff that happened years ago seemed so real, but she could barely remember what happened yesterday. Ben had always teased her, saying she had a memory like an elephant and never forgot anything. Since he'd been gone, though, everything had changed.

That day, he had been a bit late getting back with their fish and chip lunch. Usually she could time it to the minute, he was so reliable. She guessed he must have met someone he knew and stopped to chat.

"What on earth happened to you?"

"Oh, it's nothing, love. Don't fret."

He was limping and one side of his face was already coming up in a big purple bruise. There were small tears on the knees of his trousers and she could see bits of gravel stuck to bloody cuts on his skin.

"Oh, Ben. Are you sure you're all right? What on earth happened?"

"I just had a bit of a tumble. It's nothing to worry about. I just wasn't looking where I was going and I tripped over the kerb. But a nice couple helped me up and stayed with me, 'til I felt okay to walk home."

Two weeks later, he suddenly collapsed at home. One minute he was sitting in his chair, reading a book about recent archaeological digs in Southwark, the next he was lying unconscious on the floor. He had had a major stroke, and by the time the ambulance came and took him to hospital, it was too late. They could do nothing. He had lost all his faculties. He could no longer talk, walk, or eat, but his brain was still alive. It was the cruellest of endings for a good man who had always been so interested in the world. The doctors kept him alive, first in hospital, then in a nursing home, for six long months. It was a heartbreaking time, knowing that he could understand all they said to him but could not respond. It broke his girls' hearts, they had all loved their dad so much.

Dot was lost. She realised that Ben had always been there, always been her rock. His loss hit her very hard. They had been together nearly sixty years, and now she realised that, although she had often been frustrated by him, disappointed that he hadn't been able to provide her with the life she had dreamt of, none of that actually mattered. It was all just window dressing; the houses, cars, holidays, and stuff she had dreamt about was just that, mere stuff. People were all that mattered in the end, the people you loved.

After Ben was gone, Dot quickly deteriorated—so quickly that, just a few months later, she ended up in hospital after falling over once too many times. The doctors announced that, at her advanced age, she was obviously incapable of looking after herself. She would have to go into residential care. Her girls tried to fight it, saying that they would willingly care for her in their own homes, but it proved impossible to fight the hospital hierarchy once they had made their decision.

Dot was transferred to a nursing home just fifteen minutes away from her own place. For an adult who grew up as a poor child with the fear of going *"on the parish,"* or being *"sent to the workhouse,"* this was a terrible thing. She was suddenly thrust into a strange environment and living with complete strangers, many of whom were very troubled. They were troubled by the way things had turned out, troubled by the sudden loss of their independence, home, and life. Dot was bereft. She had lost not just her husband, but her home, and most of her possessions, too. Now, in the nursing home, she was living in one small bedroom—with just a bed, an armchair, and a couple of bookshelves. Every morning, she was wheeled into the big, brightly-lit lounge area, plonked into a wingback chair, and left to fester there all day, while a huge television showing some banal gameshow blasted away in the corner. None of the residents were watching it, they were mostly in a world of their own, muttering away, reminiscing about their old lives. They remembered the lives they had when they were in control of their own destiny—could wear what they wanted, go where they wanted, eat and drink what they wanted, and watch their favourite programmes on the television.

Dot ended up living in that environment for seven long years. At first, she tried to be positive, to converse with the other inhabitants and the overworked staff. Gradually, she gave up. For the first year, she kept asking her children she was going home. It was heartbreaking for her daughters, having to watch her rapid deterioration. They watched her change from the strong, feisty, loving, and opinionated woman she had been into someone they barely recognised–a quiet, sad version of her former self. She was now someone who often didn't recognise them when they visited, or who accused them of neglecting her. She claimed they never bothered to visit, even though each time she said this, they had been in just a few days earlier. She forgot *their* names, but seemed to remember people from her distant past. She recalled information about people she hadn't spoken to for years. They kept paying the rent on her house for that first year, optimistically hoping she would get better and be able to return to her own home. However, they hoped in vain. In the end, they had to admit defeat, emptying the house of all their parents' possessions– nearly sixty years' worth of belongings and memories. It was a heartbreaking time for them all.

She spent seven long years in that nursing home. She became like part of the furniture, just another sad, old soul in the corner of the room. The nursing staff came and went. They generally didn't last very long, as it was a poorly-paid, backbreaking job, and many of them could not understand why all these old people were put into care homes. In their cultures, they always cared for their elders at home, loving and respecting them until they died.

Although Dot's memory was going, she still had ambitions. She was determined to live to celebrate her 100th birthday; sadly, she only managed to make it to the grand age of 93.

She became a little more lucid in her final few weeks. She talked about her childhood, her hopes, and her dreams. She stopped talking about all the things she regretted, all the things she hadn't managed to achieve. Instead, she talked more about her family–her girls and her grandchildren.

At least her girls had managed to see a bit of the world; they had all travelled. Ann had even lived on the other side of the world for a few years and Dot had loved getting her regular letters telling of all her adventures. These were adventures that Dot would have loved to have had herself. Although at times she felt a little envious of the freedom and opportunities her girls had, in her heart, she was glad–glad that their lives were richer and fuller than hers had been.

She talked about Ben.

"I really did love him, you know. He was a good man."

THE END

REFERENCES

Meg Merrilies. A poem by John Keats (1795 -1821)

The Lion and Albert A poem by Marriott Edgar (1880-1951)
Written in the 1930s
This became famous as a monologue performed by Stanley Holloway.

Perfume from Provence A novel published in 1935 by the Honourable Lady Fortescue.

The Intelligent Woman's Guide to Socialism and Capitalism by George Bernard Shaw. Published 1928.

Heidi A novel by Johanna Spyri. Published in 1956

The Secret Garden   A novel by Frances Hodgson
                                     Burnett.
                                     Published in 1911

Uncle Tom's Cabin   A novel by Harriet
                                     Beecher Stowe.
                                     Published in 1852

AUTHOR BIOGRAPHY

Pat Backley is an English woman, who, at the age of 59, decided to become a Kiwi.

She now lives in New Zealand, and, when not writing, she loves to travel the world, walk on the beach, garden, and socialise. Pat is passionate about people, architecture, interior design, and ancestry. She always has plenty of ideas, and says she now intends to write until she dies!

Her other books are:

DAISY
THE SECOND DAISY
FROM THERE TO HERE (WITH AN AWFUL LOT IN BETWEEN)
SEVENTY YEARS WORTH OF TRAVEL
THE ABANDONED WIVES HANDBOOK

THE ANCESTORS SERIES:

VALENTINE GEORGE
LOU AND EUSTACE
DOT AND BEN

She has also contributed to several anthologies, including:

THE WARRIOR WOMEN PROJECT: A SISTERHOOD OF IMMIGRATION, RELATABLE VOICES, and LETTERS TO MY DARLING HUSBAND. She regularly writes short stories and articles for various magazines.

If you have enjoyed this book, please leave a review.

Visit her website www.patbackley.com to learn more about her and her upcoming books.